Young Love in Memphis 3:

Heart on Reserve

B. Love

Soar young girl. Soar.

www.authorblove.com
www.blovesbooks.com

Hey Guys!

In part three, they are 24 and 25. Less emphasis will be placed on Grace and Hanif because they've pretty much got it together lol, but you better believe every chapter they are in will give you life!

Prologue

In the Meantime

Vega

Jess was so nervous you'd think she was the one getting married instead of Grace. I watched as she flew around her bedroom trying to get ready for the wedding. Grace and Hanif didn't want a huge ceremony. Just something small and intimate with those closest to them.

I can't lie... this would be the first wedding I'd ever been a part of in my life... and it had a nigga thinking about my own wedding – to Jessica.

She grabbed her shoes before walking back into the bathroom. Because I knew her so well, I grabbed her bra and panties off the bed and had them in my hand when she came flying back out of the bathroom. Jess rushed over to the bed and I lifted my hand.

With a smile, she grabbed her underwear from my hand and kissed me quickly.

"You're the best, baby," she tossed over her shoulder as she went back to the bathroom.

An hour later she was walking out of the bathroom looking like the goddess she was. Her hair was completely blonde now, and it was sitting at the top of her head in a bun. The makeup she had on was so light and natural looking I could hardly see it. Grace chose gray dresses for her and B to wear. It was a long one shoulder dress with a side split. It was tight at the top, but loose at the bottom, like a toga wrap.

"How do I look?" Jess asked looking down at her feet.

My head shook as I stood and made my way over to her. She looked up at me and smiled.

"You look amazing as always, Jess. Absolutely beautiful."

"You're quite handsome yourself, young man. If Grace wasn't a nervous wreck, I'd have my way with you."

Jess wrapped her arms around my neck and bit down on her lip.

"Well, we need to leave then before you start some shit you can't finish."

Hanif

"Look at my reflection... ain't no second guessing... always be a legend... a motherfucking legend..."

The lyrics to Snoop Dogg's *Legend* were blasting. I'm sure it was a surprise to some that that was the song I chose for my niggas and I to walk down the aisle to, but that's just the type of vibe I had. I'd been listening to that shit every morning since it came out. I guess you could say it was like my motivation. It got me hype and prepared to tackle my day.

And what I was about to face... marriage... was something that I definitely needed to be prepared and motivated for. It wasn't like I was having second thoughts... I just... wanted to be the best husband and father I could be.

I was hype as hell walking down the aisle too. Well, swagging down the aisle. The whole time I got my lil step in. Hands in the air. Head bobbing. To be honest, I had a few shots of Hen to calm my nerves, so that probably was why I was acting the way I was too. My smile was wide as hell – until I got down by the Preacher and saw Grace's parents sitting on the front pew.

"The fuck y'all doing here?"

Pastor Brown put his hand on my shoulder and my eyebrows relaxed a little, although I still wanted an explanation. I was glad we decided to have an outdoors wedding. But when it came down to Grace I'd give it to anybody *any* fucking where.

"Grace sent us an invitation," her mother informed me.

I nodded and took a step towards them. Tony's arm went across my stomach, and the young nigga Vega stepped in front of me.

"It's your wedding day, OG. You want them gone let me handle it," Vega offered.

Looking over his shoulder I shook my head.

"I just got one thing to say."

He stepped to the side and Tony's arm fell to his side. I took a step towards them and leaned down to make sure they heard me and looked into my eyes.

"Grace might trust y'all and forgive y'all, but I don't. You say one thing... you do one thing... you look one way that makes her uncomfortable and I'm shooting off. Clear?"

Without waiting for an answer I stood upright and returned to my place as Snoop's lyrics said just how I felt.

"You ain't got to like it, bitch you gon' respeck it. Look me in my eyeee... motherfucking legend!!"

Lorenzo

I figured today would be an emotional day for Braille, so I wrote her a ten-page letter and made sure it would be in her mail box so she could read it tonight. One best friend was getting married today while the other was leaving for Dallas tomorrow. It would have been completely understandable if she felt alone. But she wasn't alone.

Her family was there. My family was there. Her nigga wasn't, though, and that gap had her feeling some type of way lately.

The first time I called her this morning she didn't answer. I figured she was getting ready to go or some shit so I let it slide. Tonight I decided to wait until the last minute possible to call her to give her time to get home and settled.

When I called this time she answered immediately.

"LoLo," she spoke softly.

"Baby, how you feel?"

B was quiet and I could picture her shrugging and pulling at the hem of her panties or shorts.

"I feel okay. How are you?"

"I'm good. I was a little worried about you, though. How was the wedding?"

She grew quiet again. She was fighting back tears.

"It was beautiful, LoLo. Hanif's crazy ass almost acted a fool over her parents. Then their crazy asses walked down the aisle to Snoop Dogg."

"Yea, Vega was telling me about that. I bet that was dope as hell. That's the type of shit I'm talking about."

"So, you think you gon' do something like that at our wedding?"

I blushed and licked my lips.

"If you let me."

"I don't even care. Just as long as we get married."

"Jessie packed and ready to go?"

B exhaled into the phone and my eyes closed tightly.

"Yep. We're going to have breakfast in the morning before they leave. Grace is on her honeymoon."

She exhaled loudly again.

"I'm sorry, B."

"LoLo, I miss you so fucking much, baby. I don't know how much more of this I can take."

"You don't have to take anymore, Braille. You can date whenever you decide to."

"I don't want to! I just want you!"

I scratched my forehead and gave her time to calm down.

"I know, baby. But I'm not there for you. You need somebody that can be there for you."

"Lorenzo, I'm not trying to go there with you tonight, okay?"

"Okay. Okay. Have you started on my letter yet?"

"Nah, I ain't started on that thick ass letter. I love you for that, though. I know I'm going to go to sleep with a smile on my face. Thank you, LoLo."

"It's all good. Ima let you go, though, alright?"

"No, no letting me go, but we can get off the phone, though."

I smiled and shook my head.

"Bye, crazy ass girl. I love you."

"I love you too."

Part Three

25

Vega

My grandfather told me – when you reach that climatic point in your life of having what you'd dreamed of and worked for, you never turn your back on those that helped you get it. Of course, you remove the toxic people and relationships. Those that are hindering you in any way.

But those that helped you. And rocked with you. And supported you. You give your all to them. That's exactly what I planned on doing with Jess.

At twenty-one, we set out to become millionaires in a year. By twenty-two, that's exactly what we were. Now, with me being twenty-five and her being a few months from being the same, we both were doing what we were most passionate about for our careers. Her talk show was being watched worldwide by millions. She launched a natural product beauty line. And because of all that she'd overcome in her life, she started a mentoring program for young girls that were going through some of the same things she once struggled with in Memphis.

This Jessica was the one I couldn't wait to see. To know and experience. This Jessica was loving, open, and at peace. This Jessica went to sleep and woke up with a smile on her face. This Jessica... was the one I wanted to spend the rest of my life with.

Jess Hypnotic was now being sold worldwide. I had my dark and light line like I wanted too. We were investing in businesses and real estate like we wanted to. The only thing I hadn't done yet was open my entertainment complexes, and I was waiting on my nigga to get home to do that.

Lorenzo Bush was a day away from being a free man! My nigga was about to come home! Not only was he about to come home, but we were about to fuck some shit up! We couldn't really get too lit and travel and shit because he was going to be on probation for the next eight years, but we'd take that over him being behind bars any day.

Braille had no idea he was getting out, and that's exactly how he wanted it. See… she was helping me prepare a party for Jess to propose to her, but it also served as Lorenzo's welcome home party. I couldn't wait to see both of their faces in a couple of days when their lives would be changed forever.

For the past four years we'd been going from Dallas to Memphis. I convinced Jess to take a trip home to see her girls so we could have the party in Memphis. She had no idea what I was up to as usual and it was so funny to me. Watching her pack knowing when we returned to Dallas we would be engaged… just made a nigga feel some kind of way inside.

"What's got you all smiley?" Jess asked as she grabbed her body oil and fragrance oil from the dresser.

"You. Just… thinking about you."

She put the items in her bag next to me and cut her eyes at me skeptically.

"What about me?"

"Just how much I love you."

The smile that covered her face made me smile. She straddled me and wrapped her arms around my neck.

"Did you ever think this would be our life? Maybe you always knew you'd reach this point, but did you think you would get here with me?"

Jess ran her hands down my chest and settled her arms around my waist. Her nose caressed mine and my dick grew under her immediately. I pecked her lips before grabbing her by her waist and pulling her closer to me.

"I mean… I always knew I would get this money, but I honestly thought it would be illegally. And I didn't know if I would have my life and freedom to really enjoy it. When I first saw you at the mall…"

I stopped talking and hung my head. She lifted it by my chin and smiled at me.

"What, Vega?"

"Ion want you laughing at me and shit."

"I'm not. When you first saw me… what?"

"When I first saw you... my heart literally skipped a beat. Like that junt literally paused at the sight of you. I knew then and there that you belonged to me. It was like, that motherfucker knew it belonged to you and it wanted to get out of me and into your hands. That's why I fought so hard for you. Because I knew if I remained patient with you we would get to this point. It might have taken us damn near seven years because of your ole stubborn mean ass... but you're worth it."

She bit down on her lip and pushed me down onto our bed.

"We gotta hit the road in thirty minutes," I reminded her... but that shit really became a nonfactor when she pulled her shirt over her head.

"Vega, I love you. Like... I really love you."

Jess had this goofy expression on her face like she couldn't believe her own feelings.

"You sound surprised."

My hands went up to her breasts and I squeezed gently.

"I am. There was always something about you that I found myself drawn to. Something about you I just couldn't resist. But you make me feel like... fuck it... you just make me *feel*. It takes a special man to do that. I'm glad you never gave up on me. That you were patient with me. Cause I don't know how and who I would be without you. You make me want to love and be loved by you and I don't ever want to know what it feels like to not have your love and your energy in my life."

She had no idea just how close we were to making sure she never had to experience life without me again.

"If I have my way you won't ever have to worry about losing my love and energy, Jess. Ever."

Her body lowered to mine and she gave me one of those deep kisses like only she could. The kind of kiss that let me know we weren't going to be leaving any time soon.

Jessica

Happy wasn't the right word to describe how it felt to be back in Memphis. Saying that I was happy to see my girls just didn't feel like a good enough expression. A whole three months had gone by since I last saw them and happy just didn't fit the bill.

"Okay, baby, I'm going to be back at Braille's spot to pick you up for dinner at seven tonight. Are you going to be ready?"

I looked from Braille's front door to Vega's face.

"Un huh. I'll be ready."

He rolled his eyes like he didn't believe me before walking to the trunk to grab my bag. Braille's door opened and my head shot up like a startled cat. My mouth opened and my body tensed at the sight of her. She started dancing. I started jumping up and down. And before I knew it we were running towards each other.

The struggle was real as we both tried to kiss on each other at the same time. Eventually I gave in and let her saturate my face with kisses as I giggled.

"I missed you so much, B!" I yelled squeezing her waist.

"I missed you too! I should beat your ass for making me wait this long to see you!"

"I'm sorry! My schedule has been so crazy lately, but I promise I'm going to come home more."

"Umhm," she mumbled as she released me and gave Vega a brotherly hug.

"Make sure she's ready at seven, B," Vega said before kissing her forehead and heading back to the car.

"I'll try. You know her ass slow, though."

I rolled my eyes as I grabbed my bag and she led me into her home.

Braille's house was beautiful! She earned her nursing degree and was practicing fulltime and going to school for her Masters, so her plate was definitely full. But she seemed to thoroughly enjoy her job and she never complained, so I tried to come home and visit whenever I could.

"So, what's up?" I asked as we went to her guest room to put my bag down. "What's new?"

"Shit. Israel is still harassing me about opening a store for my shirts. Like I don't already have a full plate."

"That's great, B. Why don't you want to open your own business? Your tee shirts have been doing good since we were in high school."

"It's not that I don't want to. I just really don't have the time. Between school and the split shifts I have to work at the hospital I hardly have any time to fill the orders he places for his stores on the weekends. My workload would be triple that if I opened my own store."

"Well, if you did open a store you wouldn't have to work as much. I know you love being a nurse, but it ain't nothing like having your own business and being your own boss."

"You sound like Zo."

"What is he talking about? When is he getting out?"

"He told me next month. He's on the same shit. Ready to come home and start enjoying life again. He's been investing in businesses the entire time he's been locked up, so he's really just ready to get out and blow some money. He can't travel, though. So I don't know what all he thinks he's going to be able to do in Memphis."

"That's messed up. I mean it's good that he's getting out soon. I just don't know why they gave him such a long probation sentence."

"Hell, I don't know either. Rule said he was going to talk to one of his friend's wife. Rue. She used to be D.A. and apparently she still has some type of pull. So they're going to try and see if there is any way they can have that lifted."

"That will be great. So, what do you have planned for when he gets out? Your man will be home in days, Braille. I know you're excited about that."

She sat on the edge of the bed and smiled.

"Jessica... in all honesty... like... I can't even wrap my mind around what's going to happen when he comes home. I don't know how I'm going to feel. What I'm going to do. Like... it's been so long. I just... want to be able to be in my baby's arms and not have to worry about him letting go."

I smiled as my eyes watered. Braille and Grace were two of the strongest women I'd ever known.

"Let's go before I start shedding some tears. Have you talked to baby mama today?" I asked referring to Grace.

She and Hanif already had one son – Hosea – and she was six months pregnant with their second child.

"Yea, I was on the phone with her when y'all pulled up. She's expecting us."

"Cool. Let's head out then."

Hanif

The sight of my wife sleeping peacefully made me not even want to go to work. All I wanted to do was crawl back in bed with her and sleep the day away. The past four years have been the best years of my life. Because of God. Because of her. Because of our son Hosea.

When I met Grace my soul was tortured and weary. I thought I was happy and healthy mentally, but the more I tried to help her the more I realized just how fucked up I was. Thankfully, that's behind me. And I've been spending my days happy and in peace.

I lowered myself to kiss her cheek and rub her stomach. The second I pulled my lips from her face she wrapped her arm around my neck and brought me back down to her. I smiled and kissed her again.

"I didn't mean to wake you, baby. I'm about to head out."

"Do you have to go? Can you get back in bed with me for a little while?"

"Did you have a rough night?" I asked sliding in bed behind her.

"Yes. Your daughter kicked the shit out of me practically all night."

"Why didn't you wake me up, Grace?"

"I knew you were going in this morning so I wanted you to rest. Has your mother picked up Hosea yet?"

"Yea, she came and got him about an hour ago. You want me to make you some tea or something before I go?"

"No. I've been up. I was just laying here trying to get back to sleep. Braille called me while you were in the shower. When we got off the phone Vega and Jessie were pulling up so they're going to be over soon."

I ran my hand over her stomach again as I kissed the back of her neck. She let out a quiet moan and grabbed my hand.

"Will you feel well enough to go to the party tonight?"

There was no point in me asking her that. Even if she wasn't feeling good she was going to go.

"Yes, Neef."

"Fine. Don't let them have you all over town if you don't feel up to it, Grace. I know you're excited about Jessie being home, but you need to take it easy."

"I will, Neef," she whined as she turned to face me.

A smile immediately spread across my face at the sight of hers.

"Hey," she whispered.

"Hey."

"Did you eat some of the breakfast casserole that was in the crockpot?"

"Yea. I cut it off too so you won't have to worry about that."

"Thank you, Neef. I don't know why she's making me so tired. Hosea was a breeze. I guess this means she's going to be stubborn like her damn daddy."

I smiled harder before kissing her nose.

"So, you gon' blame that on me, huh?"

"Yep."

"I'll take the blame. You have a name for her yet?"

Grace shook her head no and put her leg on top of mine.

"No. What do you think?"

"Neema."

Her eyes closed and she bit down on her lip. Her crybaby ass was about to start crying.

"Grace in Swahili," she whispered as she opened her teary eyes.

"Will that do?"

I wiped her tears away and she shook her head then nodded.

"That's perfect, Hanif. Perfect."

"Neema it is. I need to go, though. Call me if you need me."

"Will you be back in time enough to go to Jessie's party tonight?"

"Yep. I'll be here."

"Good. I love you."

"I love you too."

Unwillingly I pulled myself out of the bed after kissing her once more. For a second I just stood there and looked down at her as she tried to get her a quick nap in. Meeting her seven years ago was literally the best thing that has ever happened to me.

Period.

Grace

Three months had passed since Braille and I last saw Jessie, so we both were super excited to have her back home. Even if it was for just the weekend. Our lives were pulling us all in completely different directions.

Braille was working like crazy. Between school, nursing, and her growing tee shirt business she hardly had any free time. I don't know how she planned on juggling all of that and Zo when he finally got out, but for now… she was in straight hustle mode.

Jessie was in Dallas doing her power couple thang with Vega. Her talk show was doing exceptionally well! And every product that I could replace with her natural product line I did! It didn't matter what I was doing… when her show came on at twelve… I was watching it! Even when I was at the coffee shop. For the most part, though, I hadn't been there much.

When I graduated college I started ghostwriting for celebrities. That led to the opportunity to write a screenplay. So now, most of my time was spent at home with Hosea, writing. Like I always wanted it to be. I can honestly say, at twenty-four, just a month away from twenty-five, I'm living the life I always dreamed about. I'm doing what I love most – writing. My husband is amazing! My son is my heart. And I know when Neema arrives life will be even better.

Neema.

Grace in Swahili. Leave it up to Hanif to come up with naming her after me in such a creative and unique way.

Jessie's hand went to my stomach and she immediately pulled it back.

"I forgot how crazy your husband is. I need to get his permission before I rub your belly."

I smiled and put her hand back on my stomach. As soon as I did Neema started kicking. She was right. Hanif can be kind of crazy sometimes.

I remember when I was pregnant with Hosea and one of the customers at the coffee shop tried to rub my stomach. Hanif politely removed her hand and told her not to touch my stomach anymore. He's big on energy and he doesn't like just anyone around me and touching all on my belly.

When Hosea was born… I didn't think he was going to let anyone hold him. Eventually he simmered down and let his parents hold him. Then B and Jessie. Then Tony. Then Vega. He still doesn't like for my parents to be around Hosea and I honestly can't say that I blame him.

Since the wedding they've been trying to be cordial. Well, my mother has. My father is still so set in his ways that when he comes around he doesn't speak or anything. Just stands there until my mom is done with her visit.

Honestly, I couldn't care less either way around. Whether they came to my wedding and stepped up or not… I was good.

"Neef doesn't mind *you* guys touching my stomach. He just hates when people we don't even know comes up to me trying to rub up on me."

"They can't help it. You're the cutest pregnant lady I've ever seen, Grace. You're so small and cute. With your big ole belly. It's not really big. It just looks big because you're so small. Then your skin is already popping. But when you're pregnant it's like you have a double glow."

"Jessie, stop. You got me blushing and stuff."

"It's the truth," B added. "You're a beast, Grace. I can't remember one day where you looked sloppy during your pregnancy with Hosea. Even with you having a bad day kind of with Neema right now you look beautiful.

"Well, I don't want to be the only one of us married with kids. B, I know you're waiting for Zo. How soon after he gets out do you plan on letting him plant some seeds in you? And what about you, Jessie? The hell you and Vega waiting for?"

Braille took a sip of her water and looked at Jessie over the bottle.

"What you looking at me for?" Jessie asked her.

"I wanna hear the answer to this myself so you go first."

Jessie rolled her eyes and fought her smile.

"I'm just… waiting for him to propose I guess. I mean… I know I'm going to marry him. I'm just… waiting for him to make it official. As far as kids are concerned… when he wants to start our family we will. We've hit that financial mark we wanted to reach before we got married and started having kids, so I guess now it's just a matter of time. His timing."

Braille and I looked at each other and shook our heads. I remember Jessie being so closed up and guarded as if it was yesterday. So, to see her embracing love and marriage and family… always brings tears to my eyes.

"Now what about you?" She asked B.

"Shit, as soon as LoLo gets out we can get married and start popping babies out for all I care. After waiting seven years for him… I'm not trying to waste any more time."

"I feel you," I mumbled.

I don't know how she went an entire seven years without catching feelings for another nigga or having sex with him. There was no doubt in my mind that when Zo got out… the world would be theirs.

Lorenzo

The second my feet touched the concrete outside of the Memphis Penal Farm I fell to my knees. Seven years. Seven long years of my life had been snatched from me and given to this place because of my foolish greed.

By the grace of God, I was officially a free man. The feel of a hand on my shoulder made me shed a fear tears.

"Welcome home, nigga. Welcome home," Vega mumbled squeezing my shoulder.

I wiped my face and inhaled deeply as I stood. We hugged it out and I inhaled a deep breath.

"How does it feel to be free?" he asked me as we walked to his car.

"Mane, ask me that after I see my girl. She still has no idea that I'm out, right?"

"Right. She thinks the party tonight is just for me to propose to Jess."

"Good. I wanna shop and shit to get fly for tonight, but I don't want nobody seeing me out taking pictures and shit. I need to get her ring. I need to pick up my car. I need to close on this house at ten. I need to get my hair cut. Mane, I got too much shit to do to get ready."

"Right. Right. Well... the closing won't take long at all. Your attorney will go over the contract, you'll sign, and give them the check. I asked your realtor to make sure the selling agent had the keys at the closing, so you should be able to go to it immediately after closing. We can go to the mall in Southaven and be back in time enough to get dressed and shit and head out."

"That's cool. I'm just ready to get this shit over with."

"Cool."

When we got in his car he grabbed a box from the backseat and handed it to me.

"Preciate this," I mumbled opening the box.

It was the iPhone I asked him to grab for me.

"It's nothing. I'm just glad your ass is out finally."

"Mane, you. I'm ready to fuck some shit up now. But first... I need to do something that has been put off for far too long."

"What's that?"
"Make Braille Meadows... Braille Bush."

Braille

I was beyond excited for tonight! Finally... Vega had worked up the nerve to propose to Jessica. She had no idea what he was up to and it was hard as hell for me to hold on to this secret all day. If anyone deserved this happily ever after it was Jessica. After everything she'd gone through she deserved all of the unconditional love Vega showered her with on a daily basis and more.

Grace and Hanif made it to the party about thirty minutes after I did and Grace tried to help me finish setting up, but her swollen feet in those six inch pumps had me quickly telling her to sit her wobbly ass down somewhere.

She was cute in her blush pink flowing maxi dress. Pregnancy looked good on her. Really, any state looked good on Grace. Her hair was down to her ass now. Still jet black in color. Her gorgeous glowing cinnamon brown skin was giving me life! And those almond shaped eyes... Grace had the most beautiful innocent eyes I've ever looked into. Her cute button nose had spread a little, but I wouldn't dare tell her that.

Her and Hanif were beautiful together. And Hosea looked like a mini Hanif. And he acts just as mean and crazy as his daddy does too. I love his little bad ass, though.

By the looks I was getting I guess I looked pretty good tonight too. I tried to dress down, since tonight was about Jessie and Vega, but she insisted that I wear an outfit I don't even know why I bought. I hardly went out, and I knew I wouldn't have anywhere to wear it... but I bought it anyway. It came in handy tonight.

It was a two-piece blush pink set. The sleeveless crop top was form fitting while the skirt was sheer and flowing. It had an intricate split on the side that displayed my left leg whenever I moved. What I loved most were the pink heels that I had on. They had gold wings along the heel that were fly as fuck. Made me look like I was flying as I walked.

My hair was curled in loose waves that fell mid-back. I did a light beat on my face. And I still had both sides of my nose pierced.

Vega texted me and told me that they were pulling up to the lounge, so I walked over to Grace as quickly as I could without twisting my ankle.

"They're outside," I whispered like Jessie was nearby and knew what we were up too.

Grace squealed and grabbed my hands.

"Oh my God! I'm so excited!"

"Girl, me too! Let me go around and make sure everything is good."

I looked around to make sure everything was perfect. The vibe was chill as hell. Casey's Lounge was a naturally classy and elegant looking place, but when we asked the owner if we could rent it for the night for Vega's proposal she spared no expense with their decorations.

The doors opened and Jessie and Vega walked in looking like royalty. They both were dressed in all white. She had on a long sleeved mid-thigh low cut white dress. And when I say low cut... I mean low cut. I'm surprised Vega let her come out with it on, but his grip on her hand let me know he didn't plan on letting her out of his sight too much tonight. The cut dipped until just under her belly button, and the sides of her breasts were showing.

She looked good as hell.

Her hair was bone straight and her makeup was golden to match the gold clutch and pumps she had on.

When her eyes landed on me, Grace, and Hanif she looked at Vega skeptically. He looked so nervous I was about to laugh, but I didn't want to make it worse. Vega led her over to the center of the lounge and sat her down.

He handed her the bouquet of flowers he had for her and she smiled brightly before pulling them to her nose and smelling. Then he handed her a glass of champagne as he began to pace. I stood and sat back down quickly.

"Vega, what's going on?" she asked.

Instead of answering her he took a step back and inhaled deeply. The music faded out, and the band he hired began to play as they walked in. She looked around to see where the live music was coming from and stood, but Vega sat her back down. As if she realized what was going on she grabbed his hands and shook her head.

The band was playing the song he said described how he felt for her perfectly – Alice Smith's rendition of *I Put a Spell on You*. And I'll be damned if Alice Smith didn't start singing and walking towards them!

Grace and I grabbed each other and tried to stifle our screams. Not only was that one of Jessie's favorites songs, but Alice Smith was one of her favorite singers. And she was literally an inch away from her.

Vega kneeled and her crazy ass pushed him and tried to stand up, but he laughed and sat her back down.

"Jess, calm your crazy ass down and let me do this," he demanded resting his hands on her thighs.

Her tears started to fall as she tried to get on the floor with him. Grace and I were chuckling at the sight. She looked over at us and stuck her tongue out, and that only made it even funnier.

"Do what?" she asked cupping his face in her hands.

"You know what," he said so low we almost didn't hear him.

"Are you sure?"

"I'm positive."

Jessie nodded and sat back in her seat. Vega took a deep breath and pulled the ring box from his pocket.

"Jessica Henderson…"

"Yes!"

"Let the nigga ask you first!" I yelled pointing my finger at her.

Grace elbowed me in my stomach and I apologized.

Vega shook his head and chuckled.

"Jessica Henderson…" he shook his head again and grabbed her hand. After placing it over his heart he continued. "It belongs to you. Always has. I trust you with it, and every other part of me. Every other part of my life. This road for us hasn't been easy, but it's been real. And it's been full of love. And fun. And passion. And growth. You're my best fucking friend. At times my worst enemy, but only to bring out the best in me. For us. We've gained so much over the past four years, and it's time for us to make this official. So…"

He opened the box and Grace and I stood.

"I love you with all of me, Jess. Will you marry me?"

"What took you so long?"

She asked snatching the ring from his hand and putting it on.

"I need to hear you say it, Jess." His voice was so soft and low. So vulnerable. It brought tears to my eyes.

Jessie kissed his lips sweetly and quickly before falling to her knees before him. Her arms wrapped around his neck and she bit down on her lip.

"Of course I will marry you. I love you."

"Awwwwww," Grace and I sung simultaneously.

"Yay!"

"Congratulations!"

"About time!"

We yelled.

Jessie looked over at us and smiled as Vega helped her to her feet. His arms wrapped around her and they kissed again as Alice began to sing *Fool for You*.

Grace handed me a piece of tissue and I wiped my face.

"This is so great," I mumbled more to myself than her.

"Isn't it though… I always knew…"

Her voice faded out. So did Alice's singing. So did the bands playing. I saw something… someone… out of the corner of my eye. Someone that looked too much like Lorenzo. But it couldn't have been Lorenzo. He had another month to do. *No*. There was no way Lorenzo was standing in the same building as me.

I closed my eyes and swallowed hardly as my stomach plummeted. As chills pierced my skin. As my underarms and palms began to sweat. As my heart began to palpitate.

"B…"

Tears slid down my cheeks immediately. This… this couldn't be real. I had to be hallucinating. Hearing things. There was no way Lorenzo was here.

"Look at me," Lorenzo ordered softly.

His hands covered my cheeks and my breath hitched in my chest. I covered his wrists with my hands and shook my head as more tears fell.

"Braille… open your eyes and look at me."

"I can't," I sobbed holding his wrists tighter. "You can't be real. You can't be here. This has to be a dream."

"I'm here, baby, and I promise I will never leave you again. Look at me."

I looked to the right of me... and Vega and Jessie were hugged up as they looked at us. I looked behind me... and Grace and Hanif were smiling at me. Lorenzo's hand cupped my cheek and he turned my face around. My eyes closed and he chuckled.

"Braille, look at me, crazy ass girl. I'm here, baby. I'm here."

With a long and deep inhale, I opened my eyes and met Lorenzo's. He licked his lips and bit down on the bottom one. A smile covered my face as tears poured from my eyes. He used his thumbs to wipe them away.

When he was done he pulled me into his chest and I whispered, "Welcome home, baby."

Lorenzo

I was nervous as hell during Vega's proposal. Nervous for him and for myself because when he was done it would be on me. The second my eyes landed on Braille it felt like my heart fell to the soles of my shoes.

She looked so damn beautiful.

Yea, she'd been visiting a nigga and shit... but it was something about seeing her outside of jail that made me really see her. *Really* see her. Every new and little detail about her. Like how her hair had grown to the middle of her back now. How her eyes were kind of shaped like a sideways S. How all of her eyelashes were long and they all curled up perfectly... except one over each of her eyes. There was always one lash over each eye that never curled. How the beauty mark under her right eye matched the one under my left eye.

I wanted to celebrate Vega and Jessie's engagement, but I wanted my baby to myself. I had seven years of absence to make up for. Braille thought when I got out we would go house and car shopping together for me, but because I got out early I had Vega to pick up the gray Noble M6OO from Rule's car lot that I wanted. That wasn't going to be my every day car, because niggas are quick to hate and try to take what they want, but it would definitely be my stunt car.

Since it was dark I couldn't really see B against the car like I wanted to, but I couldn't wait to see her and those gray eyes posted up on my car in the morning.

The entire time I drove we were rubbing on each other. Kissing at red lights. At one point I had my finger so deep in that pussy she was coming all over my seat. That was cool, though. She'd be the only person riding shotgun with me in it.

When we pulled up to my new home, the home I was praying she would move into, she looked at me skeptically.

"LoLo, whose house is this?"

With a smile, I unbuckled my seatbelt and looked over at her.

"Sit out here for a second, okay?"

"What the hell are you up to?"

I kissed her lips softly and moaned as I pulled away. Four years without the pussy was four years too many. But more than that... I just wanted to be able to hold my baby and not have to worry about having to let her go.

I want to wake up next to her and go to sleep with her in my arms.

Squeeze her ass and run my fingers through her hair.

Grip her neck while she looks up at me with those beautiful eyes.

"Just wait out here for a second, B. Don't give me no shit about it either."

"Fine. Hurry up."

She rolled her eyes at me and fought back a smile and all I could do was thank God for finally being free to be with her. I went into the house and lit the candles and incense I set up, then went back outside to get her.

We stepped into the house and she immediately looked up at me.

"LoLo, whose house is this?"

"Mine. Yours. Ours."

"Ours?"

"Yea. You want me to live by myself after not having you for seven years?"

"But I'm already renting a house."

"Rent it to someone else until your lease is up."

"How... and when did you even have the time to buy this?"

"Vega. He's been bringing me pictures and shit to look at. When I got out today I closed on it before heading to Southaven to shop."

"You've had a long and busy day, huh?"

"You have no idea. I'm tired as hell. I've literally been ripping and running all damn day since I got out, but being here with you makes it all worth it. I haven't had time to get any furniture. Honestly, I want you to. I want you to decorate every room. I just... wanted us to spend our first night together here."

"So... this is... our home?"

Braille looked up at me and smiled.

"It is. You wanna look around?"

"Right now... I just want you, LoLo."

I nodded and led her upstairs to our bedroom. When she saw the pallet I made she laughed. I stopped by Walmart when Vega and I were headed back to Memphis and picked up some candles, incense, silk rose petals, a couple of pillows, and some comforters.

"Really, LoLo? You gon' have my damn knees black and sore by tomorrow on this hard ass floor."

"Long as you know," I mumbled huskily as I slapped her ass.

"Not that I don't appreciate your effort... I promise I do... but for what I want to do to you... we need a bed. Can we go to my place and then go shopping for furniture in the morning?"

She had her hands on my chest... looking up into my eyes... I couldn't refuse her even if I wanted to.

I groaned and gave in. "Fine, but we're staying here when we get the furniture in."

"I can't wait. This place is beautiful, LoLo. How many bedrooms?"

"Four," I answered as I walked over to the candles and began to blow them out.

"You mean to tell me the first thing you did when you got out was start building for our future?"

I looked back at her skeptically.

"Of course. What else would I be doing?"

She shrugged and lowered her head.

"I missed you so much. I'm so glad you're home. I still can't believe you're here with me."

"Well I am, and I ain't going nowhere."

"Thank you for this. I can't believe this is happening. You're home. And you're here. And this is our home."

She shook her head and covered her face. A few seconds passed and her shoulders were shaking from her crying so hard. I ran my hand down my face and released a hard breath as I walked over to her. Braille wrapped her arms around me and pulled me close.

"Cut all that crying out, girl. We good now."

I took her face into my hands and pulled her from my chest so she could look into my eyes.

"I love you, Braille."

"I love you too. Now let's go so you can make love to me."

Braille

As much as Lorenzo and I craved each other you'd think we would be ripping each other's clothes off, but we weren't. The second we made it back to my place… into my bedroom… we took our time with each other. He stripped me of my clothing. Then I removed his. When we were completely naked and unashamed, we crawled into the middle of my bed.

His body was hovering over mine as he caressed every part of my body he could reach. But he didn't rush to come inside of me. Nor did we ruin the moment with too much talking. For a while… all we did was caress and look at each other.

It all still seemed so unreal. LoLo was here. In my bed with me. After seven years. He didn't go see his family as soon as he got out. He didn't go to the strip club, or to a party with his niggas. No, he went and signed for us a house. Got him a pretty ass car. Then went shopping for something to wear.

Who does that shit?

Lorenzo fucking Bush!

Just the thought had me blushing and closing my eyes.

"What's up with you?" he asked with a smile.

I ran my hand down the back of his head and neck as I answered him.

"Just thinking about you. Having you here with me. How setting shit up for us was your main priority as soon as you got out. How blessed I am to have you."

"I told you I would give you the world for rocking with me, and I meant that shit. This is nothing. I'm going to get us some matching cars tomorrow. You deserve more than a house and a ring and…"

"Wait… a ring? You didn't give me a ring."

He smiled and bit down on my neck.

"I didn't?"

"No, Lorenzo. You didn't."

"I thought I did."

"Lorenzo. You didn't."

"Mane, I know I gave you a ring as soon as I saw you."

"No you didn't, LoLo."

"Are you su-"

"LoLo! You ain't give me no damn ring!"

He chuckled and kissed my irritation away momentarily, but I pushed him away and crossed my arms over my chest.

"What ring?"

Instead of answering me with words, LoLo stood and walked over to his pants. He pulled a small black box out and slowly walked over to the bed. I sat up and pulled my knees to my chest. Lorenzo sat next to me and grabbed my hand.

"I can understand if you want to take some time to get to know me all over again, B, but you're it for me. I want to spend the rest of my life with you. As your husband. The father of your children. Your provider. Your protector. Your best friend. I want to be everything to you that you've been to me."

He opened the box and I literally gasped. Like... my breath literally caught in my chest. It wasn't because it was the biggest and flashiest ring I'd ever seen. It was because it was the ring I tried on seven years ago when we went to Nashville. The ring we used to have my finger sized. I started crying all over again.

"You mean it was still there?" I asked in disbelief.

"Nah. I... bought it when we first went. The next morning while you were still sleep I went back to the mall. I've had it in a safety deposit box since then. Of course I can get you a bigger diamond now but... I just... figured this could at least be a good engagement ring."

"You mean you've known all this time that you wanted to marry me?"

"Braille, I knew I wanted you the second I laid eyes on you. All I've been doing is waiting for time to catch up with my heart and how I've always felt about you. We could've gotten married when we were eighteen if it were up to me."

"Ask me."

"What?"

"Ask me to marry you."

His smile was small as he grabbed my hand and stood. I chuckled at the sight of us. Butt naked in the middle of my floor. Lorenzo kneeled and looked up into my eyes. I couldn't get enough of him. All I wanted to do was touch him. My fingers ran down his cheek as he spoke.

"Baby, you know I want you." His voice was so low and desperate it pulled a moan out of me. His grip on my hand tightened. "And I need you. I... I love you. So, will you marry me, Braille?"

"Yes. I will marry you."

His face lit up, like he couldn't believe it.

"You will?"

"Duh!"

Lorenzo pulled me into a bear hug and lifted me into the air. I squealed as I fell back onto the bed. He slid the ring onto my finger and looked down at me for a few seconds before his mouth covered mine for the deepest kiss he'd ever given me.

The calmness and exploration that filled us before was gone and replaced with urgency and hunger. Each place his mouth landed on my body felt like it was consumed by fire. His nails dug into my thighs as he spread my legs apart.

"You don't know how much I've missed this," he mumbled into my pussy before using the full length of his tongue to lick from my ass hole to the tip of my clit.

I wanted to please him just as much as he wanted to please me, so we got into a 69 position that I failed at horribly when his mouth closed over my clit. It was so hard to focus with his sucking. His slurping. His biting. His licking. His fingers. His moaning. It was too fucking much. I took him into my mouth and tried to focus but the tightening of my walls had me lifting my head again.

Lorenzo laughed as he slapped my ass.

"You gon' do something while you down there, or nah?"

"I'm trying," I whined.

My tongue ran over the head of his dick, then I took as much of him into my mouth as I possibly could. He moaned again and squeezed my ass.

"Fuck this shit," he muttered while grabbing my ankle and flipping me over on my back.

His body covered mine and he entered me with one long, slow, and deep stroke. My arm wrapped around his neck as I pulled him closer to me. His lips captured mine and he opened them with his tongue.

"I missed you," he confessed with his lips pressed to mine.

"I missed you too. So much."

"You really gon' marry me?"

"Yes, baby."

"I can't believe you really waited for me."

I opened my eyes and looked into his. They were watery. As if he was fighting back tears. He closed them quickly and began to stroke me, but I grabbed his face and forced him to look in my eyes. The second he did a tear fell from his. Lifting my head slightly, I kissed his tear away and moaned as his pelvis brushed against my clit.

My head fell into the pillow as he pushed and pulled himself out of me consistently. As my pussy slathered his dick with my cream.

"You got that creamy shit," he moaned pulling out of me. "You know it's been a while. I don't know how long I'm gonna last this first round."

I smiled and grabbed his dick to put him back inside of me.

"I don't care. We can go again. Just fill me."

It felt as if every second that passed he was stroking me deeply. Not missing a beat. Not missing a stroke. Moaning in my ear. Biting down on my neck. Whispering how good my pussy felt. How much he missed it. How much he missed me.

"Fuuuck, LoLo," I grunted.

His strokes were getting harder. Faster. He pulled out, and I pulled him right back in by wrapping my legs around his waist tightly.

"Don't pull out," I begged.

"Braille..."

He started stroking me again. Faster. Deeper. His hands wrapped around my neck as he lifted himself from me. My pussy tightened around him.

"Shit, B."

My legs started to tremble.

"I'm about to cum," he warned me.

"Me too. Please don't stop."

"B... I'm about to cum."

"I don't care. Don't stop stroking me, please."

He moaned and lowered his body onto mine.

"B..."

My arms wrapped around his neck. His lips covered mine as he lifted me off of the bed slightly. Hitting me even deeper. I moaned into his mouth as I heated. Trembled. Came. And just like the first time... he came right along with me.

Lorenzo

A smile covered my face as soon as I felt the sun's rays on my skin. This was what I'd been dreaming about for years. Waking up holding B. Waking up with her body on top of mine. Waking up free. Waking up in a king sized bed. Waking up when the fuck I wanted to and being able to do what the fuck I wanted to do.

I kissed the top of her head and ran my fingers through her hair.

"Why you up so early?" She asked with sleep heavy in her voice.

"I get up when the sun gets up."

"But we just went to sleep."

I smiled again. We hadn't been too long went to sleep. After going a few rounds we ate and went a few more. Just the thought had me running my hands up and down her back. I wouldn't force her to let me inside now, though. She earned a break. But I didn't have to ask because she straddled me and slid down on the dick so slow and sexy I could've came just from that.

"You ain't had enough yet?" I asked gripping her waist.

"Not even close."

"Get that shit then."

Braille smiled and lifted herself, then dropped back down on me. Taking all of me in. She was wetting my dick already as her mouth opened and her head flung back. With one hand on her breast and the other on her waist I controlled her movements and made her ride me the way I wanted her to.

She was coming and falling onto my chest instantly.

"Get your ass back up," I ordered with a smile.

"I need a break."

"Nah, you wanted this. Finish me off."

She mushed my face playfully before turning her back to me and sliding back down on my dick. Her pace sped up as she rode me backwards. First, she was going straight up and down and I could handle that shit. Then, she gripped the sheets and leaned forward. Making sure I went as deep as I could. With her back arched perfectly. Had my ass moaning and smacking her ass with my toes curling up.

"Get that shit, baby. Ride that dick."

I grabbed a handful of her hair and she moaned as her pussy tightened against me. As the ridges of her g-spot became more and more defined.

"LoLo…"

"Cum, baby."

And she did. And so did I. And that's when I realized we hadn't been using protection. My mind immediately went back to the abortion. When she was composed, B laid back down next to me. I turned sideways and looked at her.

"You on birth control?"

"I haven't had a reason to get on birth control. I planned on getting on some before you got home, but you're a month early."

I sighed and wrapped my hand around her neck.

"What we gon' do? We need to get you a plan B pill or something?"

She bit down on her lip and shrugged.

"If you want to. I…" She closed her mouth and twisted it to the side.

"You what?"

A tear slid down her cheek and I knew she was thinking about the abortion too. I hated not being there for her at that moment. Really, that's the only thing I regret out of this whole thing. Not being there for her when she needed me most.

In the softest voice I'd ever heard her use she said, "I wanna have your baby. If you want me to."

"Of course I do. But I want it to be when you're ready."

"I am ready."

"Are you sure?"

"Yes."

I smiled and pulled her face to mine for a kiss. She giggled when she felt my dick growing against her.

"Already, LoLo?"

"Yep. All fucking ready."

Braille

Waking up to my baby gave me such life. He told me that as soon as he got out he was going to propose, but I didn't believe him. I thought he would take some time to be single and wild out before he committed himself to me like that.

But this nigga buys us a house. Cars. Matching cars. Proposes to me. Literally his first day out. I couldn't even put into words how his actions had me feeling. Every time he did some shit yesterday and today all I wanted to do was spread my legs for him. I know sex ain't everything, but I swear it was the best way for me to express my love for him at this moment.

After we made love I don't know how many times this morning, I fixed breakfast and we went to Rule's car lot. LoLo purchased himself a Cadillac Escalade, because he said he refused to drive his Noble in Memphis on a daily basis, and me a Cadillac Sedan. Like there was anything wrong with the car I already had. His response… just sell that hoe.

Swear I love his crazy ass.

Once we put our cars at our new home we went furniture shopping. After that he wanted to find me another ring before he met up with his folks, but I told him the ring he gave me last night was perfect. I wouldn't trade it for anything else in the world.

It wasn't until we got back to my house so I could meet up with my landlord about subletting it that I realized I had completely forgotten about my shift at the hospital.

"Shit!" I yelled rummaging through my purse for my phone.

"What's wrong?" LoLo asked.

"I completely forgot about my shift at work. My boss is going to kill me."

"What time were you supposed to be there?"

"Eight."

"This morning?"

I nodded and scrolled down until I found Nancy's name.

"B… it's four."

"I know," I mumbled putting the phone to my ear, but he removed it and disconnected the call. "LoLo…"

"Let's... talk about this for a second before you call."

"Talk about what?"

Lorenzo put my phone between us on the couch and took my hands into his.

"We're getting married soon, right?"

"Right."

"And you're moving into the new house as soon as the furniture arrives, right?"

"Right."

"And we going half on a baby, right?"

"Right."

"How do you think you're going to be a wife, mother, full time nurse, full time student, and have your tee shirt business on the side?"

My eyes lowered as I bit on my top lip. I hadn't really thought about that. My schedule was so full to keep me from missing him. I didn't think about how having a full plate would hinder my personal life when he got out.

Of course my priority was going to be him and our kids, but I didn't want to completely lose my identity in him just because he was home.

"You want me to quit?"

"I would never ask you to quit, Braille. Not that you even have to work. I've been investing in businesses for the last seven years, so you know what kind of bank we're sitting on. You've been wanting to be a nurse before you knew I existed. I'm just saying... maybe you need to scale back on some things. I'm home now, and call me selfish, but I want as much of your time as I can possibly have. I'm not going to tell or ask you to do anything, but that you make sure your priorities are in line."

He handed me my phone and kissed my forehead before standing.

"I'm about to go to my mom's crib to kick it with them for a little while. What time will you be back home tonight?"

"I don't know. I guess after class. My last class ends at nine."

He nodded and kissed my forehead again.

"I'll see you then."

I nodded and sat back in my seat. *Make sure my priorities are in line?* I called Nancy and apologized for my absence and not calling in properly and she excused me. Said that she had someone covering my shift for the day so I didn't have to worry about coming in. Asked me if everything was okay, since I've never called in or missed a shift. I told her my baby was home and she all but forced me to take my paid vacation time to get reacquainted with him.

I agreed only because I figured two weeks away from the hospital would give me time to figure out how in the hell I planned on juggling everything already on my plate, along with LoLo and the fact that we were trying to start our family.

When I ended the call with her I called Jessie and asked her to meet up with me for dinner. Her schedule was just as hectic as mine, so I figured between her and Grace she would understand my dilemma most. Grace's plate was full with being a wife and mother first. There was no doubt about that.

Then she made time to write from home. The café was her last priority, and she went in whenever she had free time. So had I talked to her about it she would just tell me to quit and let Lorenzo provide for us while I did my tee shirt business and the wife and mama thing. That was cool... but I wasn't sure if it was exactly what I wanted.

Jessie agreed to meet up with me. Now, *I* wanted to go to an actual restaurant and sit down, but she wanted some Dixie Queen because they don't have one in Dallas. So she went through the drive through and grabbed us something to eat. Since I didn't know when she would be back in Memphis I told her to meet me at the new house so she could see it.

Our furniture hadn't arrived yet, but the pallet LoLo made for me the night before was still there so we ate there and talked.

"What's wrong?" she asked as she popped a seasoned fry into her mouth. "Zo getting on your nerves already?" She couldn't even get it out good because she was smiling and trying to eat at the same time.

I mugged her but it quickly turned into a smile.

"No, I'm... I'm so glad he's home. It's just... I feel like I didn't have time to prepare."

"Prepare for what exactly?"

"His return. Like... you know I had every detail of my day and life planned. Work. School. Tee shirts. Spending time with my niece and nephew. Spending time with Grace and you. That's been my routine. He gets out, proposes, buys us a house and cars, and it's like... everything stopped because of him. I forgot about my shift at the hospital today. I don't want to go to class tonight. All I want to do is lay up with him."

Her hand covered my knee and she squeezed it softly.

"That's perfectly understandable. You haven't had him for seven years, Braille. Hell, if Vega's schedule conflicts with mine for two or more days straight, I'm ready to shut everything down for a day or two to reconnect with him. It's natural that you want to spend all of your free time with him."

"But I can't. Like... I can't just put my life on hold for him. I can't not work and go to school just because he's home. I just... feel like..."

"You're going to lose yourself in him?"

I nodded and smiled softly.

"I've learned how to be without him. I don't want him to come back and I just... unravel."

"Have you talked to him about it?"

"Not fully. He told me I need make sure my priorities are straight." I chuckled and shook my head. "He doesn't expect me to quit and drop everything for him, but I think he does want me to make sure I put him first. Especially when we get married. And we've been going at it without any protection so I know I'm going to end up pregnant."

She pushed her food to the side and sat Indian style.

"There's a fairly simple way for us to figure this out."

"What's that?"

"Do you have some paper and a pen in your purse? If not, I have a journal in mine."

I grabbed my purse and pulled my mini notebook out.

"At the top I want you to write *My Priorities*."

I looked at her skeptically. She was about to go into talk show host mode on me. Jessie smiled and pointed at my paper.

"Write it, B."

"Alright."

I did as she said and looked at her for her next instruction.

"I'm going to ask you a question. I want you to answer honestly. Don't say what you think you should say, but how you honestly feel."

"Okay."

"Between school, work, your tee shirt business, and Lorenzo… which one can you not live without?"

With no hesitation I replied, "Lorenzo."

"Between school, work, and your tee shirt business… which one do you need to give your energy to most?"

"School."

"Between work and your tee shirt business which one gives you the most satisfaction?"

"Work."

"Okay… so your priorities are Zo, school, the hospital, and your tee shirt business. Your schedule needs to revolve around those things in that order. Maybe you can just work part time at the hospital and do your tee shirts on weekends only."

"Or do away with it completely. Or hire someone to press them for me while I come up with the slogans and designs."

"There you go. Now you're thinking. If you hire some help that will definitely free up some of your time. How would you feel about working part time at the hospital?"

"I could see that working. Maybe I'll cut back on the hours, or continue my twelve hour shifts and just work certain days." I had that light bulb feeling. "I have an idea." My fingers started scribbling quickly.

Jessie leaned forward and tried to understand, but the shorthand I was doing made that practically impossible.

"Okay. I have class three days out of the week. I have one semester left. Mondays, Wednesdays, and Fridays I have class. So, I will work at the hospital on Tuesdays and Thursdays. Weekends will be reserved for LoLo and family. I'll hire someone to press my shirts, and I will only work on new designs for one to two hours a day on my school days. By the end of the semester my schedule will be even more free…"

"Your ass will be good and pregnant by then."

"Shut up. It'll be even freer then and I can reevaluate my schedule then and maybe pick up more shifts at the hospital, or just rearrange my schedule so that I can work two or three days straight and have the rest of the week free for Zo, the potential baby, family, and traveling."

"Sounds like a plan to me."

She smiled and I frowned.

"I'm glad you're here. I miss you so much, Jessie."

"I miss you too. Sometimes I wish we could stay here more."

"Me too."

We both sighed heavily and smiled.

"Well... we almost married ladies na!" She exclaimed in her *The Color Purple* voice. "What us gon' do?"

I laughed and returned my attention to my food.

"Girl... I have no clue. You and Vega have practically been married the whole time so it won't be anything new for y'all. This shit with LoLo, though..."

"You'll be fine. You guys will get everything taken care of. Just work together and communicate."

I nodded and licked my lips... praying it would really be that simple.

Vega

I couldn't return to Memphis and not get a fat burger from Reese's BBQ. Most people who lived in Memphis had a love hate relationship with our city. Sometimes we hated it and wanted to leave... but there was something about the culture. The soul. The music. The hustle. The language. It just... was like nothing you could find anywhere else.

I rapped with Rule the last time I was here, so his brother Power wanted to kick shit with me before I left this time. Power and Rule kind of became mentors for young niggas in Memphis. Especially those of us that used to be in the streets. Sometimes it seemed like I was a mix of both of them. I was crazy like Rule, but on some deep and soulful, emotional type shit like Power.

When I pulled up to Reese's, I saw his car outside and couldn't help but smile. A nigga tried to be on time most of the time, but my ass was always late! After I ordered my food I went over to his table. We dapped it up and I sat across from him.

"What up, young nigga? I heard you finally making an honest woman out of Jessie."

Just the mention of her name and our future together had me blushing.

"Hell yea. Her ass finally on some act right."

"That's what's up. I'm proud of y'all, man. You, Zo, and Canon."

"Preciate that. We trying."

"Nah, y'all doing. Ain't no trying about it."

My heart filled with pride as I nodded. Hearing that from him was like hearing that from my big brother.

"How's Elle doing?"

"She's doing good. Crazy as ever."

"Her and Cam got that shit honest. And Braille acts just like them."

"Yea, it runs in their blood. She's good, though."

"And what about the kids?"

"Man... they're doing good. Growing up so fast. When I was your age I knew I wanted marriage and shit, but I didn't think it would happen so soon. Now, Elle, Power Jr., and Ellie are my whole fucking world. I can't even think of anything good that happened in my life before them."

I leaned into the table, wanting to ask him something that had been bothering me, but I held my tongue. He sensed it because he leaned into the table as well.

"What's on your mind?"

My fingers raked over the top of my head as I shook my head.

"Just... thinking. Me and Jessie accomplished what we set out to do, you know? We got our million. We've gone beyond that over the years. She has her talk show. I got my dark and light line of liquor added to Jess Hypnotic. We're investing in businesses and real estate... but it's just... something is missing."

"Something like what?"

I shrugged and sat back in my seat.

"Ion know. It's like, in Dallas... we're all about the hustle, but when we come home, it's family here. Our entire vibe and priority is different. When we come back to Memphis she's so much happier because her family is here. Her best friends are here. Now that Zo is out I really don't want to go back to Dallas. I've been waiting on him to get out so we could go into business together for these entertainment complexes. It just... seems like... Dallas was a season for us and I'm getting over that shit."

"How does Jessie feel? She wanna come home?"

"I don't know. She doesn't talk about it. It's probably just me."

"I mean... what's stopping y'all from coming home more? Y'all got a house here and a house in Dallas. Why don't y'all just make this where you spend the most time? Y'all can just go back to Dallas when she needs to tape her shows."

My food was ready so I went and got it before I replied.

"Ion know. They say home is where the heart is and I swear I'm ready to come home. Ain't nothing like Memphis. For real. I complain about it when I'm here I ain't gon' lie, but... I miss this shit."

"You young niggas overthink shit and make it more difficult than it really is. Let me show you how you handle your woman. Give me your phone."

I smiled and pulled my phone from my pocket. After I unlocked it I slid it to him.

"Jessie is first in your favorites, right?"

"Right."

Power pulled her number up and called her, then put the call on speakerphone.

"Yes, baby?" She answered.

I smiled and crossed my arms over my chest.

"This ain't baby. This Power."

"Heeeeey! Where y'all at?"

"Reese's."

"Reese's?! Why y'all ain't let me come? I want a fat burger."

"Cause I knew your ass was gon' get something from Dixie Queen. Haven't you?" I questioned.

She was quiet for a second before mumbling, "Yes."

Power smiled and shook his head.

"Listen, Jessie. My young nigga is stressing over here about some simple shit that I need you to clear up for him."

"Uh oh. What's wrong?"

"What's most important to you?"

"God, my family, and Vega. Come our wedding day God and Vega above all else."

I smiled and ran my hands down my face.

"So there's nothing you wouldn't do to make sure he's happy and at peace, right?"

"Absolutely."

"Well, I need you to tell him that. And that he can communicate with you about anything because for some reason he doesn't think he can. Probably just the man and pride in him."

"Vega?"

"Huh?"

"What's up? You know you can talk to me about anything."

"I know. I just... Ion know."

"What is it, baby?"

"I wanna come back home."

She was quiet for a few seconds and Power and I just stared at the phone. Then she ended the call and Facetimed me. I grabbed the phone and held it up to my face.

"Jess..."

"You mean you want to move back to Memphis? Permanently?"

"Well... not permanently. I do want to spend most of our time here. I know we'll have to be in Dallas for your taping, but I really do miss it here. And Zo is out now..."

"Why didn't you just tell me? I wanna come back home too. Me and B were just talking about that."

"For real?"

"Yep."

"Well... we'll talk about it."

"Boy, get off my phone. You know whatever you want to do as long as it doesn't go against God and my personal wellbeing I'm down for. I thought something was seriously wrong with you. Talking about some you wanna come back home."

"Mane, get off my phone. Always messing with me."

"Whatever. When you coming home? I miss you."

"I'll be headed that way when I leave here. You know me, Canon, and Zo going out tonight, though."

"Umhm, let Canon get y'all in trouble if you want to."

"Bye, Jess."

"Bye."

I disconnected the call, cleaned my hands with some sanitizer, said my grace, and took a big ass bite out of my burger. Power just looked at me and shook his head.

"What?" I asked with a mouth full of food. Jess' bad eating habits were rubbing off on me.

"You look like a completely different person now that that is off your chest."

"Shit, I feel like one. Feel like a weight has been lifted off of my shoulders."

"See... that's the great thing about marriage. It's a partnership. *It's about two people navigating through life as one.* Now... you will always have somebody that you can lean on, build with, seek peace, love, respect and support in. But you have to always communicate with her. She can't fulfill your needs if you don't make them clear to her. And it's obvious she has absolutely no problem taking care of your needs."

"She doesn't. I guess I just always want to put her first. She's living her dream in Dallas. I didn't want to put a damper on that."

"That's very noble of you, but at the end of the day... if you aren't taking care of yourself and making sure you're satisfied you won't be any good to her or anyone else. It's about balance and fulfilling each other's needs. You can't hold the weight of taking care of hers while neglecting yours. Give them to her. That's her job as your wife now. Just like it's your job to satisfy hers. There's love and power in that exchange when it's done correctly."

"That makes sense. I 'preciate you for meeting with me."

"It's all love. Just make sure you take the knowledge I'm giving you and apply it to your life as wisdom. Knowledge is knowing a tomato is a fruit. Wisdom is not putting it in your fruit salad."

I chuckled and shook my head. Him and Rule were always on some deep and philosophical shit. Swear I was glad to be home.

Jessica

Vega's random confession about wanting to come back home made my day! I was *just* talking to Braille about how much I missed being home and wished we could be here more. Look at God! We would have to go back to Dallas to tape my show... but shit... when I got off the phone with him my mogul senses started tingling.

With the platform I have why can't I start my own production company right here in Memphis? If I'm going to be the next Oprah I need to follow in her footsteps! She has OWN. Jessie needs to have JESS. I want to go beyond a talk show. I needs to have my own network!

I couldn't wait until he got home so we could talk about my idea, but knowing him he was going to be drunk and out of it tonight. So, I decided to just wait until tomorrow or when we got back to Dallas to tell him about it.

After I left Braille and Lorenzo's beautiful home I headed to Christina's school to surprise her. I picked her up and we went to get a mani/pedi. Christina was starting to look so much like my sister it's crazy. That is so bittersweet. I look at her and I see Jasmine and I love that, but it makes me so sad sometimes because she's not really here.

We left the nail shop and was headed for Kroger to grab some rolls for our family dinner when I heard a little girl call my name. I knew the voice instantly. Isabell. Israel and Layyah's daughter. Israel. Cameron's brother. Cameron.

I turned around and my eyes landed on Isabell. She ran to me as quickly as her six-year-old legs would allow her to and hugged my waist tightly.

"Well, hey, Bell!" I yelled kissing the top of her head a few times.

"Jessie! Where have you been? I haven't seen you in forever!"

I kissed her again and squeezed her a little tighter.

"I've been in Dallas, honey."

"I thought you said I could come and visit you?"

"You can come whenever you want."

"Okay."

"Who are you here with?"

"Uncle Cam."

My eyes closed at the sound of his name. We hadn't seen each other in a while. After he told me about his marriage proposal and baby I stopped going around when I knew he would be there. Not because I wanted him back, but because I just didn't want to see that.

I looked up and locked eyes with him. He'd cut his damn hair! It was cut into a low fade, but everything else about him was the same. He still looked just as beautiful. I smiled as he walked over to us.

"Hey, stranger," he mumbled unwrapping Isabell's arms from around me and pulling me into his.

It took me a second to register the fact that he was hugging me, but when it did I hugged him back.

"Hey, Cam. Why in the world did you cut your hair?"

I ran my hands down his head as he held on to my waist and looked into my eyes. He didn't answer me right away. He just... looked at me and smiled.

"What?" I asked.

His smile widened.

"Cameron..."

"You're full. You're a full moon right now. I can see it in your eyes. There's no pain or anger there. They're happy. Shining. Even your voice is lighter and happier."

I smiled and ran my hands down his arms as I looked from Isabell to Christina. They stopped around his wrists.

"I am," I admitted softly. "I'm in a really good space. On all levels."

"That's really good, Jessie. Really good. I'm really happy for you. Proud of you."

I blushed and lowered my head.

"Thanks, Cam."

"Aunty Jessie, can we get some cherries when we go in the store too? Uncle Jabari ate all mine up!"

I chuckled and turned my attention to Christina. That sounded about right. Jabari was always going over somebody's house eating their fruit.

"We can get whatever you want, baby."

"I won't hold you. I just wanted to come and speak," Cameron said as he released me.

I hadn't even realized he was still holding me until he let go.

"How's the wife and the baby? Have you had any more?" I asked.

"She's good. The baby is good. Well she's not a baby anymore. We haven't had any more yet, but we definitely want to."

"That's good. You have any pictures?"

"Really?"

"Of course. I wanna see what a mini Cameron looks like."

He smiled and pulled his phone from his pocket. He didn't have to go to his photos. His home screen was a picture of all three of them together.

"Oh my God, Cam. She has your hair. She's beautiful. You're going to have a problem on your hands with her."

"I know. That's why I'm not in a rush to have another one."

I looked at him and smiled.

"Your wife is beautiful too. She looks like a sweetheart."

"She is. She's great. What's up with you, though? Besides being on my TV every time I cut it on."

We took a step back from each other and I smiled.

"Not too much. Just living. Oh! I'm engaged."

"Word? To who?"

"Vega."

He nodded his approval and looked down at the ring on my hand.

"That's great, Jessie. I knew he was something special to you when you chose him over me."

"Cameron…"

"I didn't mean anything by that, girl. Relax."

I nodded and took a deep breath.

"Well, I've got to get the rolls to my mama's house. She's having a family dinner tonight," I informed him.

"Cool. Well it was great seeing you, Jessie. You look amazing."

"Thank you, Cam. It was great seeing you as well."

Cameron stepped towards me and placed a light kiss on my forehead before whispering, "It's good to see you shine," in my ear.

I looked into his eyes and nodded slowly and softly as I took a step back.

"Later, Jessie."

I nodded again and grabbed Christina's hand.

"Aunty Jessie, who was that?" She asked.

"Uh… an old friend, Chrissy. An old friend."

Vega

Jess expected me to end my night with my niggas late as hell and to be drunk when I came home, but I knew she was missing me just like I was missing her so I came home early. When I walked into the home we shared in Memphis and found her in the middle of our bed she damn near jumped out of her skin.

She got on her hands and knees and smiled widely.

"Baby! What are you doing back already?" she asked as I walked over to the bed.

Jess crawled to the edge of it and I kissed her while running my fingers down her cheek. I ran my nose over hers and kissed her again quickly before stepping back.

"I just wanted to get back to you. How was dinner with your folks?"

She shrugged and returned to her place in the middle of the bed as I undressed.

"It was cool. I told them about us getting married."

"Oh yea? What they say?"

"About time."

I chuckled and got on top of the covers with her.

"I guess it is, huh?"

Jess straddled me and ran her hands down my chest.

"I saw Cameron today."

It was such an unexpected confession it took me a while to respond. I grabbed her wrists and she looked into my eyes.

"Where?"

"At Kroger."

"How did that go?"

She shrugged and lowered herself to kiss my chest. My dick grew against my wishes.

"It was... weird, but cool."

"Why was it weird?"

She shrugged again ran her fingers around my nipples. Like she didn't know that shit made my dick jump. Her ass was trying to distract me. And it was working. I put her on the side of me and faced her.

"It just was."

"How, Jessica?"

Instead of answering me she just looked into my eyes. I was about to get out the bed, but she grabbed my arm.

"Where you going?"

"To take a shower."

"Right now?"

"You ain't saying shit. Fuck you want me to do?"

"Are you mad?"

"Nah. Is there a reason for me to be mad?"

"No."

"Jessica... just tell me what happened."

"We just talked for a couple of minutes. It was weird because... I don't know. It's like... the way he looks at me. He sees me in a way that no one else does. He saw something in me that no one else could. When he saw me today... he was happy to see me because he saw that in me. What he knew was already there. Pulled from beneath the depths of me."

I nodded and ran my tongue over my teeth as I inhaled a slow breath. The fuck she mean the way he looks at her? That he saw something no one else saw? If I didn't see anything in her crazy ass she wouldn't be in Dallas living her dreams. I'm the cause of that shit! Not him!

"Well, that's good, baby," I mumbled before kissing her forehead and rolling out of bed.

"That's good? That's all you have to say?"

"Yea."

I grabbed my bag and went through it. Looking for my black boxers. Couldn't find them for the life of me.

"Vega... is... what's... are you..."

"It's cool, Jessica."

I went over to the dresser to see if I'd put them in one of my drawers.

"Your black boxers are in the bathroom on the sink. I figured you'd want to take a shower when you got back so I put them and the rest of your stuff in there already."

Disappointment. Disbelief. Hurt. All of that shit was slowly consuming me. I couldn't even look at her. I just went into the bathroom silently.

"Vega, why are you shutting down on me like this? I don't understand what's wrong."

"Did you not hear what you just said, Jessica?"

"No. Obviously. Just tell me what I did wrong."

"You didn't do anything wrong, baby."

"You said I could talk to you about anything."

"And I meant that."

"So why do I feel like you're mad at me?"

"I'm not mad."

My heart is aching, but I'm not mad.

"Then what is it?"

"Nothing. I'm just tired and... I need to take a shower and unwind."

"Okay."

I closed the door behind me, cut the shower on, and sat on the toilet. This was not how shit was supposed to be. Not after the day I proposed. I ain't never been the insecure type, but when it comes down to her I find myself questioning if I'm really enough.

And every time Cameron's light skinned ass pops back up it's some shit.

I spend seven years trying to show her that I accept her. That I see her for who she is. That I'm capable of giving her what she wants and needs. That she can totally be herself with me. That I would never try to change her. That I love her unconditionally. And after all of that... she still thinks *he's* the only one who ever saw the real her.

How the fuck am I supposed to compete with that?

If she can't see that after all of this time... I just... I give up.

I was hoping by the end of my shower that she'd be sleep, but she was up. Hugged up with a pillow. Waiting for me. I avoided her eyes as I grabbed my phone from the bedside table.

"Vega..."

"It's fine, Jessica."

"Then why do you keep calling me that?"

"That's your name."

"No. Not to you. It's Jess. It's always Jess. Not Jessie. Not fucking Jessica. Just Jess. Just Jess."

The crack in her voice made me feel even worse.

"Baby... it's fine. Really."

"You're lying."

I finally looked at her and noticed her glossy eyes. After sitting my phone down, I took a step towards the bed.

"Fine. I feel some type of way right now."

"Thank you. Why?"

"Because it seems like no matter how hard I love on you... no matter how hard I go for you... no matter what I do for you... there's always going to be this connection with him that you have that I can't compete or compare to. And I get that shit. I get that he was there for you during a very difficult time in your life. But for you to sit there and tell me to my face that he's the only person that saw you. The real you. That's like a slap to my fucking face."

"Vega, that's not what I meant..."

"But that's exactly what you said. That's *exactly* what you said. And I'm sorry but that shit is bothering the fuck out of me right now."

Tears started sliding down her cheeks and her voice was low as she muttered, "I'm sorry."

"You don't have to be sorry. That's... how you feel and you're entitled to that. It's... not your problem. It's mine."

"I didn't... Vega, I'm sorry. I know you see me. It's just..."

"You owe me no explanations Jessi-" I stopped myself and groaned. "I need to go get a drink."

She watched as I dressed, but I kept my eyes from her.

"Vega, I know you see me. He was the first. But you're the last. I didn't mean it like that."

I snatched my phone and wallet from the table and put them in my pocket. Can't believe I rushed home to deal with this shit.

I kissed her forehead and mumbled, "Don't wait up," on my way out of the room.

Jessica

He told me not to wait up but I did. He didn't come back home until four in the morning. And even then he didn't come back to our bedroom. He crashed on the couch downstairs and went straight to sleep.

I felt bad as hell. When I said that shit about Cam being the only person to see me... *why the fuck did I say that shit?* Cameron had a way of talking to me and looking at me that made me feel like I've never been talked to and looked at before. That's... just... the... energy... that he has. And even with him having that type of energy I would never trade in Vega for Cameron. Ever. Period. Not even on our worst days.

I love Vega with all of my being. And I know I hurt him with my momentary slipup. There's no excuses for it. No explanations. I fucked up. And I hurt him.

After he fell asleep I went downstairs and put a pillow under his head and a comforter on top of him. Then I went to sleep myself.

When I woke up he was knocked out, so I cooked his favorite breakfast – biscuits with crumbled sausage in white gravy, and a side of fruit. He woke up and showered but left before eating. He didn't even say anything to me.

I know he wasn't trying to be mean or hurtful. If anything... he was trying to *avoid* being mean and hurtful. But that was hurting me most. I ate alone, then showered and prepared to spend my day alone.

Braille was more than likely under Zo. Grace was doing the family thing with Hanif and Hosea. And here I was fucking up my marriage before it even began.

Me: I love you. I'm sorry. When you're ready to talk I'm here.

I read that text for the fifth time since I'd sent it two hours ago. He hadn't replied yet. There was only one person that I felt could help me get through to him – Power. Power and Rule understood Vega in ways his own father hadn't tried to.

They had the same kind of stubborn, emotional spirit. If I needed to break through that, they would be able to help me. I called Elle out of respect and asked her if I could talk to Power. A few seconds later his laughter filled the phone as he spoke.

"What's up, Jessie?"

"I fucked up. Royally."

His laughing stopped immediately as he told Elle to take Ellie in the front room.

"What happened?"

"I... I don't know. I mean... I saw Cameron yesterday."

"Oh shit."

"It was harmless. I told Vega and I said some shit about Cam looking at me like he's the only person who sees me."

"Is that how you really feel?"

"Of course not. Cam just... he has a way of getting under my skin, but I didn't mean that. Vega accepts and loves me unconditionally. Cameron never did that. I don't know. I hurt him and that's the last thing I've ever wanted to do. He feels like loving me has been in vain. And he has every right to feel that way. But I don't want to lose him, Power. I don't want him to feel like I don't appreciate him."

My tears were beginning to fall so I stopped talking before I started sobbing.

"Have you told him any of this?"

"He won't talk to me. He left the house this morning and didn't say shit to me. I texted him but he isn't replying."

I wiped my tears and snot and chuckled quietly at myself. I never thought I'd be this deep in him.

"Hold on. Let me call him and see what I can do. Don't say shit, Jessie."

"I won't."

Power merged the calls and I put my phone on mute.

"What's up, OG?" Vega spoke.

My heart practically melted at the sound of his voice.

"Where you at, young nigga?"

"At my folk's house."

"Go see about your woman."

Vega was quiet. Too quiet. For too long.

"I... can't. Not right now. I just... need some space."

"What do you think space is going to do? What I tell you when I saw you?"

"Communicate."

"Space, time, distance... that's only going to make it worse. You need to handle this shit. Now."

"I can't give her what she needs, man."

"Yes you can," I sobbed until I remembered he couldn't hear me.

I disconnected the call, ran up to our bedroom, and grabbed my purse and keys. If he didn't want to come home... I was going to go to him.

Vega

When I pulled up at the house and saw that Jess' car was missing I started to leave and go back to my folk's house, but I promised Power that I would try to work this shit out with her so I went inside and waited for her.

A few minutes later she walked in looking like a sad puppy. I nodded for her to come and sit next to me and she did.

"Where you been?" I asked.

"Looking for you."

"I just needed some space, Jess."

"Ain't no space, nigga. We work shit out around here."

As much as I didn't want to I smiled and placed my hand on her thigh. Her lips brushed against my cheek softly.

"I hope you brought your shovel, if you wanna dig deep down in my soul, babe. Cause loving me is a motherfucker... hard to hold on to something so cold," she whispered into my ear.

I turned my face so that our lips were touching slightly as she continued to sing *Break Me* by Mayaeni.

Her hand caressed my cheek and I bit down on my lip in frustration. I loved this girl too much. Too fucking much.

"I need you to break me, baby. Break me, baby."

Jess straddled me and I wrapped my arms around her involuntarily.

"I'm sorry, Vega. I'm going to be completely honest with you. Cameron has a way of getting under my skin. He's like my mother. They can make me feel so good or so bad about myself. It's like there is no in between. I wasn't... I didn't mean that shit last night. Okay? I know you see me. I know you do. I don't want him. I want you. I love you. I want to marry you. I know you see me, baby. I'm sorry."

"Jess..."

"You wanna know the first time I knew you saw me?"

I pressed my head into the couch and looked at the ceiling.

"When?"

"When we were supposed to go out on our first date. The day I broke up with him. I told you about my past and him and… you didn't take advantage of my vulnerability. You didn't judge me. You weren't trying to just be on some fuck shit. You listened to me and you understood me. And you gave me exactly what I needed at that time. No matter how much I ignored it and tried to fight it, Vega, you had me at that moment.

You saw me. And I was yours. You don't have to try and compete with him. You don't have to try to compare yourself to him or what we have with what I had with him. Vega, I don't want him. All I want is you. All I've wanted is you."

She grabbed my face and forced me to look at her.

"Do you hear me?"

"Yea, I hear you."

"Do you believe me?"

"I do."

"Do you forgive me?"

"Yes, Jess."

"Do you trust my feelings for you?"

"I do."

"You still wanna marry me?"

"Well…"

She punched the shit out of my chest and I laughed as I grabbed her and pulled her into me for a hug.

"I'm just playing, baby. Of course I want to marry you still. You ain't getting rid of me that easily. I was just… in my feelings. I felt like… he connected with you on a deeper level than I did. You know I'm crazy about you. That just fucked with me."

"But he doesn't. I promise he doesn't. You're the reason I'm living my dreams today. If you didn't see me… I don't know where I'd be and what I'd be doing right now. If no one else sees me I know you do. I'm so sorry for making you doubt that."

"It's cool."

I wrapped her arms around my neck and she kissed me.

"I love you, Vega. I'm sorry."

"I love you too. Stop apologizing."

"Okay. Grace wants to go shopping today since we're leaving tomorrow. Oh yea, I wanted to talk to you about some shit."

Jess sat next to me and I pulled her leg on my lap.

"What?"

"I was just thinking… with the platform I have now, maybe I wouldn't have to do my show in Dallas. Why can't I start my own show here? Why can't I be in control of every aspect of my show? If I want to get my Oprah on I have to start being more hands on."

"What you saying… like… you want your own production company? Your own network or some shit?"

"That's exactly what I'm talking about."

"So like, instead of OWN it would be JESS?"

She looked at me and smiled as tears filled her eyes.

"What's wrong, baby?"

"This. How we work. How you get me. I don't even have to say shit and you just… get it. You get me. You think you have to compete with a memory? With an ex? Vega, we go beyond that. We're on some other realm shit. Cameron can't compare to this. No other man has or ever will. I don't give a fuck what I say or how I say it don't *ever* question that."

I sat closer to the edge of the couch and pulled her onto me.

"Get your ass over here and sit on this dick."

Jessica

Vega and I were returning to Dallas tomorrow, so we were looking forward to the little get together Zo and B were having tonight. I met up with Grace at the mall to try and find them a house warming gift, but we ended up buying things for Hosea and Neema before deciding to go to Walmart and get the newly engaged couple a few flat screen TV's.

Who would have guessed Grace would be the first to get married and have kids? I just knew Zo and B would get married before us all. But now... Braille and I were engaged at the same damn time! And to best friends at that!

I smiled quietly at the thought.

"What you over there thinking about?" Grace asked from across the table.

We'd stopped to grab something to eat at O'Charley's. Really, I just liked to go for the rolls, but whatever.

"Us. How much we've changed and grown over the years. The fact that you're freaking married with kids, and B and I are engaged at the same time!"

"To best friends!"

"Right!"

We both chuckled and shook our heads.

"Have you and Vega started planning the wedding yet?"

My smile dropped slightly. We hadn't really had time to. Before we could even get to that point I almost messed it up with my reckless mouth. Honestly, we hadn't even talked about the wedding or even marriage since he proposed. I just figured we would when we got back to Dallas.

"Nah."

Her head tilted forward slightly and she twisted her mouth up.

"As excited as you were after he proposed you mean to tell me you guys haven't done any planning at all?"

"Nah."

"Why not, Jessie?"

I shrugged and took a big bite out of my roll to avoid answering her, but that really wasn't a good excuse because I had a bad habit of talking with food in my mouth anyway.

"Why not?" She repeated.

"I may have... temporarily... caused... a little... eh... friction."

"How? What did you do?"

"I may have... eh... said something about Cameron after I saw him."

She grabbed the corner of the table and leaned into it.

"You saw Cam? When? Where? What happened? Start from the beginning."

After I told her everything that happened she sat back in her seat and let out a heavy breath.

"The hell would you say that shit for, Jessie?"

"Girl... I don't know. I'm telling you... it's like... I don't know. Cameron has this way of..."

"I know I know. Getting under your skin. But why?"

"Hell if I know."

"Do you still love him? Like *love him* love him?"

I lowered my head and shook it.

"I love him, but I'm not *in* love with him. I'm in love with Vega."

"Do you... wish you could be with Cam?"

"Of course not. I can't explain it, Grace. All I know is... he came into my life when my heart was closed off, and he reopened it. So it's like... he can get inside of it and fuck with it in ways that no one else can. I don't mean to let him, and I'm sure he doesn't even know that he can. But he does."

"I just have one question... forget his wife. Forget Vega. If the roads were all clear for you to be with Cam... would you?"

After scratching the back of my neck I looked at her and thought about it. Really thought about it. Thought about it in a way that I never had before.

Would I?

"The new Jessie. The whole and free Jessie. Would she be with Cam right now?" Grace continued.

I smiled and leaned into the table.

"See… that's just it… like… Vega and I have become one in such a way that I can't really see my life without him in it. I can't see myself with another man. Not even in a hypothetical sense. When I think of love and a life partner… all I see is Vega."

"Well, if that's the case… there's no doubt in my mind that what you experience with Cameron is simply… the same thing I felt for Andy."

My mouth opened partially in shock. She smiled and nodded to my silent question of if she was serious.

"Explain," I mumbled.

"Because Andy provided an escape for me I felt obligated to be with him. To be there for him. To put him above myself. The only reason I left him was because I reached my breaking point. I know the same thing would have happened with you and Cam had you not met Vega. You more than likely would have stayed in a committed relationship with him because that's what he wanted… because he was there for you when you needed someone most… and you would have been miserable.

The only difference is that Cam was a good guy and Andy was crazy as hell. But we both were in crazy mental and emotional states when we met them. We both felt rescued by them. We both felt consumed by our relationships with them. I felt so protective of Andy because of how he helped me that even after all he'd put me through… when I found out that he was indeed mentally ill… I still wanted to be there for him.

No matter how unhealthy it would have been for me. Thankfully I had Hanif to pull me out of that. What you feel for Cameron… it's thankfulness. It's appreciation. It's respect. It's an unnoticed obligation to a man that made you feel when everything else around you made you numb. But what you have with Vega… that's priceless, Jessie. Protect that with all you have.

I know you're cool with Layyah and she's married to Cameron's brother… but protect what you have with Vega at all costs. Let me let you in on something I've learned from being with Hanif. My relationship with him was completely different than my relationship with Andy.

Men gravitate towards women they think they are going to be successful at loving. Even though they love a challenge, they aren't going to invest their time and energy into something they believe is going to fail. A man will chase a guarded woman or a nagging and difficult woman for so long before he gives up on her completely.

He loses interest if he feels as if he can't meet her needs and expectations. If he can't give her the love she needs. It doesn't matter how much he loves and wants her... *it's against his nature to consistently put himself in the position to be devalued and feel like a failure.*

I don't care if you have to completely ignore Cameron when you see him. If you have to stop going around Israel and Layyah's home. You need to do what you have to do to make sure Vega knows he is successful in loving you. That you value and appreciate and respect him. That he has what he needs within him to meet your expectations and give you what you want and need.

This battle between him and Vega in your heart can't go into your marriage. There should be no doubt in his mind that he's the only man that resides there. And that's up to you to make sure he knows that. I don't care what you had with Cameron and how good he made you feel... that shit needs to end. Now."

I sat back in my seat and closed my eyes as Vega's words to Power replayed in my mind.

I can't give her what she needs, man.

Tears immediately filled my eyes. The last thing I wanted to do was make him feel like he failed at loving me. And that's exactly what I'd been doing when it came down to Cam. Me telling him that I chose him instead of Cameron meant nothing when I turned back around and said shit like he was the only one that saw me. That he was the one that made me feel and love again. Yes, that may have been true... but that was in the past. He was my first, but Vega is my now. My last. And he's who I need to boast on.

"Grace, you're my baby and I love spending time with you, but I need to get to my man."

She smiled and grabbed another roll.

"I wouldn't have it any other way."

Hanif

Grace was such a naturally sweet and innocent woman that sometimes... most times... I forgot that she could be just as fucking savage as me. But I was reminded of that side of her when we took Hosea to Chuck E Cheese – along with everyone else nearby.

I was standing in line to get some more tokens when I saw a boy who was a little bigger approach him. I called Grace's name to get her attention and she nodded, but didn't make her way over. We both watched their exchange from a slight distance.

Then, the older boy pushed Hosea and tried to take his tickets. Grace tried to walk over and stop it, but I wanted to see if the boxing lessons Hosea had been taking for the past year was worth it. My Pops had my brother Hosea and I in a boxing ring when we were two. I started Hosea at three. Now he was encountering his first bully.

The first person that felt entitled to take what he had. What they wanted. I loathed people who felt entitled to shit they didn't deserve. People like that are the reasons my brother and best friend were murdered.

As I expected, Hosea hit the bully with a left right combo to his jaws and like the little man he was growing up to be, Hosea didn't swing on him when he fell down. He gave him time to get up. By the time he did his mother was rushing over.

Quick enough to keep his little bad ass from getting further whooped, but her ass wasn't close enough to keep him from trying to take something that wasn't his. Ain't no telling how many other kids he'd bullied out of their tickets and tokens. He picked the right one to try this time, though.

Grace quickly wobbled her pregnant ass over and I sighed as I put the money in my pocket and walked over.

"Is there a problem here?" I asked before Grace could even open her mouth to speak.

"Hell yea there's a problem here! You didn't see your son just attack my child?" the bully's mother damn near yelled.

I shrugged and pulled Hosea behind me next to Grace.

"Yea, but I also saw your child push and try to snatch something that didn't belong to him from my sons' hand."

"You think I give a fuck about him trying to take some damn tickets? He put his hands on Rodney!"

She tried to reach around me and grab Hosea but Grace punched the right side of her face and grabbed her legs when she pulled her hands to her face for protection. As soon as she fell on her back, Grace put her foot on her neck.

"Hanif, did this bitch just reach for my son?" Grace asked me in disbelief.

I nodded and inhaled deeply.

"Yea, but you're pregnant, so you need to let that shit go, baby."

Grace looked down at her for a few seconds as she struggled to remove Grace's foot from her neck.

"If these security guards come over here, Grace, I'm going to jail."

"I don't want you to go to jail, Neef," she whined.

"Then let her go and let's go."

With a pout, Grace removed her foot, grabbed Hosea's hand, and stormed off. The whole time I drove home I kept looking over at her smiling. She was heated. Hosea had no problem taking care of himself, and she know I wasn't gon' let nothing happen to him, but just the fact that that bitch even tried to get at him made her ass see red.

I wanted to get her out of her funk, so instead of taking Hosea home with us I took him to my folk's house so I could pamper her. Really, I wanted her to go to a spa or some shit but she wanted to go home instead.

As soon as we got back, she plopped down in the middle of the couch and called Jessie and B to rant. I let her for a little while before making her get off the phone to take a shower. When she was done I rubbed her body down with that body butter shit she bought from Jessie. Then I soaked her swollen feet and massaged them until she was falling asleep sitting up.

I carried her to the bed and tried to pull myself up but she wouldn't let me.

"Get in bed with me, Neef."

A smile covered my face as she slowly opened her eyes and looked at me.

"I thought you were sleep?"

"I was just resting my eyes."

"Umhm, get on your side of the bed."

I'd put her in mine to avoid this, but it looked like I wasn't going to get away with that this time.

"Neef?"

"Yes, baby?"

She pushed herself deeper into my chest and put my hand between her thighs.

"Why are you so wet, Grace?"

"Because my husband just catered me to sleep. Make love to me."

"You sure?"

My hand cupped her breast as I licked and kissed her neck.

"I'm positive."

"Like this?" I asked pushing her left leg up towards her stomach.

"Yes, baby. Just like this."

I stood and removed my clothes before sliding back inside of the bed. Behind my wife. Behind my rider. Behind the woman I was anxious to grow old with.

Grace

When my mother asked if she could go to the next appointment I had to check on Neema I was surprised. I told her to let me check with Neef first, and she agreed, but made sure to let me know that she really wanted to come.

So, Hanif decided to let her come – and he wouldn't. Mean ass. I'll give my mother a point of credit... since the wedding she'd been trying to be more involved in my life. And when Hosea came into the world she gave him the love and nurture she never gave me.

Now she was all into going to doctor's appointments and what not. It was... a little weird. I didn't mean to keep staring at her, but I just wanted to know her deal. Like was she dying or something? Was she trying to get close to me because she needed something? There just had to be a reason she was into me and my life all of a sudden.

"Ma?" I called into the silence between us.

"Yes, Grace?"

"Why are you here?"

She gave me a small knowing smile before hanging her head. When she lifted it she came and stood next to me.

"The night of your prom, Hanif loved and cared for you more than your father ever loved and cared for me. After thirty years of marriage. He loved and cared for you more than your own parents did. I didn't realize just how little I gave you until I witnessed someone give you so much."

She grabbed my hand and caressed it with her thumb.

"That started a shift within me. A shift that led to me coming from under the rule of your father's thumb. That led to me wanting to reconcile with you and be in my grandchildren's lives. That led to me serving him with those papers."

I removed my hand from hers and turned slightly to face her.

"Divorce papers?"

She nodded and smiled.

"When?"

"Two weeks ago."

"Has he... is he going to sign?"

"He did. For a moment I... wondered if he would fight for me... for us... but he didn't. He just... looked at me, grabbed the papers, and signed."

"So what now? Where are you living? Do you need help with anything?"

"Now... I live and love. Simple as that. No I don't need anything from you. Just your forgiveness and permission to remain in your life."

I grabbed her hand and smiled. I'd lost all hope when it came down to my father... but I was more than willing to accept this late and hopeful relationship that was building between my mother and I.

"Sure. I'd like that."

She nodded and wiped the tear that was slowly sliding my cheek. Dr. Anderson walked in and greeted us both. My mother tried to return to her seat but I held her hand tighter and she stayed next to me.

"I hear this is your first visit with Grace?" Dr. Anderson asked.

My mother nodded and smiled.

"Well... how's about we let you hear your granddaughter's heartbeat?"

"Can I?"

"Absolutely."

Dr. Anderson rubbed the gel on my stomach and just a few seconds later Neema's strong heartbeat filled the room. My mother used her free hand to cover her mouth as tears filled her eyes. I'd seen her cry so many times I thought maybe something was wrong. I mean... that's the only time she ever showed any emotion in the past.

"You okay?" I asked her.

"I'm... perfect, baby. These are tears of joy. Definitely tears of joy."

She leaned down and kissed my forehead and I felt myself letting out a few happy tears of my own.

Lorenzo

I wanted to kick it with everybody close to me when I got out... but Braille... I craved her. It was like... when I was with other people... all I could think about was her. All I wanted to feel was her. All I wanted to see was her. I wanted to see her pussy covering my dick with her cream. Then I wanted to just leave... and let her stay on me. So I could see, feel, and smell her remains on me until I made my way back to her.

Life goes on, and I know we can't be up under each other every second of every day, but I'll be damned if I don't try to make that happen.

Wife: LoLo.

My legs opened immediately and I smiled as I looked down at her text. When I left her this morning she was still asleep. Knowing her, she reached out for me, and when she didn't feel me she grabbed her phone to text me. We'd gotten so close over the last few days that we could literally feel when the other's presence was in and out of the house.

Me: I'll be home in a few. Meeting with your brother in law.

Wife: He's about to be your brother soon.

Me: How soon? We need to set a date, B.

Wife: Can we start planning today? I've got one more week on vacation before I have to go to work and I want to get as much planned as I can.

Me: Of course. Whatever you want.

Actually, I was meeting with Rule to see if he was able to pull some strings and get my probation sentence waived. One of his close friends, Malik, was married to the former D.A. of Memphis. She still had some clout in the city, so they were supposed to be seeing what they could work out for me.

I'd just given the system seven years of my life. I was ready to live and be free. Being tied down to Memphis for the next eight years of my life felt like another level of torture.

Building a black wall street here was still at the top of my goal list, and with Vega and Jessie moving back to Memphis we were definitely going into business here together... but shit... I wanted to be able to up and leave whenever I wanted to. I wanted to show my baby the world. I wanted to make love to her on islands, in planes, in caves... wherever her heart desired.

I hated feeling confined and tied down.

The only thing I wanted to be tied down by was a wedding ring on my finger.
And that's it.

Rule finished his call and came back into his man cave. He lit up, took a hit, and passed me the blunt like we did in the old days. I declined it because a part of my probation was that I not smoke weed or be caught with it. His ass knew that.

When I first got out we had a heart to heart about my intentions with Braille. I felt bad as hell about getting locked up and leaving her, and I knew his ass would make me pay for it... but it was like... he respected me. I guess because I didn't try to force her to wait for me. And as soon as I was out I proposed and prepared to right my wrong of leaving her.

"Well..." I pried.

He smiled and sat back in his seat.

"I was talking to Vega. You know him and Jessie do real estate investing. I was talking to him about investing in properties out of state."

My face felt like it was dry as fuck. It must have been because his smile widened before he continued.

"He was telling me that you wanted to buy a private island and name it after Braille when your probation was up. I looked into that shit and it's really not as expensive as I thought it would be. I might look into something like that for the kids. Something they can have when Camryn and I are long gone."

Honestly, it wasn't very expensive at all. I was looking at one a few miles from the Gulf Coast... just outside of Florida that I wanted to buy. Really, I wanted that to be our little getaway spot. I wanted it to be where we got married. I wanted it to be a place that was just for us.

But this probation and not being able to travel thing was making all of that seem impossible. So, I figured I would just buy it and rent it out to travelers until Braille and I could explore it together.

"Yea, I found one that I want, but shit... this probation..."

"Is no longer a factor. Buy that shit. Take my sister there. And make sure she has the time of her life."

I sat up in my seat and turned my face slightly so that my ear was more towards his mouth.

"What you saying, Rule?"

"I'm saying… your probation was waived. Before you did your seven years you had nothing on your record. You shouldn't have been given the max with that being your first charge. The judge just wanted to make an example of you. You served your time with no incidents. Rue was able to pull some strings with the current D.A. You're free. No probation. You're free."

My hands covered my mouth as I closed my eyes and inhaled deeply. *Thank God.*

"Thanks, bruh," I mumbled as I stood.

"You know I got y'all."

He stood and we shook it up before I left. Braille was going to melt when I told her about this. When I got to my car I pulled my phone out and called Vega.

"What up, nigga?" he answered.

"Shit. Aye, how soon can you make that deal on that island happen?"

"I mean… you paying cash so as long as they don't have any offers on that hoe we can close it in a day or two like we did your house. Just depends on how soon we can get everything finalized. How soon we can get a hold of the regulations and if it needs any type of clearances or inspections. This would be the first one that I've dealt with, so unless they have a different set of rules that don't apply to other types of property it can be done in a matter of days."

"Make that shit happen. Soon."

Braille

To busy myself while I waited for LoLo, I finished up the last of my designs for my tee shirts. When I finished this last batch, I decided that I would just call it quits. Really, I didn't plan on doing it for this long. I started it in high school as a hustle to fund me. It's never been something that I've been passionate about. And now that I have so many other things on my plate it's become more of a means to keep me busy than anything else.

Since he's free, though, I have no need for it anymore.

I emailed the designs to Israel, Cameron's brother, and he called me immediately.

"Sup, Is?"

"Uh, you talked to Jessie lately?"

"Not for a couple of days, why?"

"I've been trying to get in touch with her."

"Well, she's been taping shows back to back because they're trying to leave Dallas. What's up?"

"I need to talk to her... about Cameron."

I groaned silently as my leg began to shake.

"What about him?"

"He's been kind of reckless since he last saw her."

"What do you mean?"

"Just... having some thoughts a married man with a kid shouldn't be having. About Jessie. I need to talk to her. See if she can talk to him."

"Ummm I'll see if I can get in touch with her. What do you want her to do... call him?"

"Whatever she can. I know she's engaged and everything, but he needs this. Seeing her messed him all up."

"I'll see what I can do. I can't make any promises, though."

"That's cool. I preciate you. Those designs are dope by the way."

I smiled as LoLo entered our bedroom.

"Thank you. Thank you so much for giving me the opportunity to sell my designs in your stores."

"No problem. Glad I could help."

"Alright, talk to you later."

"Aight."

I disconnected the call and took my man in from head to toe. My God, I missed him.

"Who was that?" He asked as he removed his shoes.

"Israel."

"He giving you a hard time about quitting with the tee shirts?"

"Not at all. He completely understands. We talked so long because he wants me to try and get in touch with Jessie."

Lorenzo came and sat next to me.

"For what?"

"He wants her to talk to Cameron."

"For what?"

I shrugged and put my head on his shoulder.

"Ion know. Something about he's been thinking about her or something. I don't know. Ima text her, but I know she's probably not going to call."

"Mane, Vega will eat that mane up. He better gon' on with that."

"I don't think Cam would try anything. I think he's holding it in and that's why Israel is worried."

"Well, do what you gotta do as far as that is concerned then pack you a couple of bags."

I turned to the side to better see him.

"Pack some bags? For what?"

"We're going to Miami for a few days. And when this deal is done I have somewhere very special I want to take you."

I grabbed his hands and squeezed lightly.

"So... this means... you're not on probation?"

"No, baby. I'm a free man on all sides."

"Yaassssss!"

I jumped into his lap and hugged his neck tightly. All he did was chuckle and hold me just the same.

Vega

Today I prepared for my last party in Dallas. I'd spent the day making sure everybody was on the same page. When I promoted exclusive parties with over two hundred attendees I hired Canon for security, so the last thing I did before making my way home to my future wife was go through the building and all exits with him.

I texted Jess as I normally did when I was on my way, and she greeted me at the door with a shot of dark Jess Hypnotic. After I chugged it down she grabbed my hand and led me to the bathroom. I smiled at the sight. Jessica Henderson Freeman was the only woman I'd let put me in a bath. Not just a bath... but a bath filled with essential oils, dried flowers, and fruit.

I just straight up refused to let her put me in a bubble bath, but the first time she talked me into an oil bath I was hooked. Now, she gave me one once or twice a month... or when her ass got on my nerves and was trying to make up for it.

She must have thought I still felt some type of way about the Cameron shit, but I was over it by the time we left Memphis. I wasn't going to tell her that right now, though. Not while she was feeding a nigga's soul like this.

I watched her intently as she removed every piece of my clothing. Once I was inside of the tub she lit up a blunt and sat on the toilet while I soaked. Putting the blunt to my lips so I could take a hit every once in a while. The water grew cold, so I stood and showered. When I was done I stepped out and she stood.

The second she was within reach I took her face into my hands and tried to kiss her, but she pulled away and said, "Not yet," so soft and sexy yet desperate.

Made my dick stand at attention immediately.

Jess massaged her oil moisturizer into my skin from my neck to my feet then patted the excess water and oil from my skin with a towel. She left and returned with my boxers and house shoes. She didn't just put the shoes in front of me so I could step into them. No, she got on her fucking knees, lifted my ankles, and put my feet into the shoes.

Then her ass had the nerve to look up at me and wink. I grabbed her by her hair and pulled her lips to mine. She let me kiss her for a second, but the moment I slid my hand under my shirt that she was wearing she pulled herself away.

"Not yet," she repeated.

I let out a hard breath and nodded.

Her fingers intertwined with mine and she led me into our bedroom. She sat me down on the edge of the bed and put both of her hands on the sides of me. Her face was so close to mine I could have easily kissed her, but I didn't want her to pull away again so I sat there and just... let her have her way with me.

She licked her lips, licking mine in the process, and caressed my nose with hers. I pulled my arms behind my back to keep from touching her.

"You know I respect you, Vega... don't you?"

She looked down my body slowly before looking into my eyes. To be honest... I couldn't even answer her right away. My mouth opened... but she had me so captivated... I couldn't even put words together. So I nodded instead.

"And you know that I value you. And appreciate you, right?"

I nodded again. She kissed my lips softly and wrapped her hands around my neck. Her thumbs grazed my cheeks as she stared at my lips.

"And I love you. More than I've loved anyone else. Just as much as I love myself. You believe that... don't you?"

I nodded and put my left cheek on her right one.

"And... you know that you give me everything I want and need. You... go above and beyond anything I've ever expected from a man. From love. I love the way you love me, Vega. You know that... right?"

I nodded, wrapped my arms around her waist, and sat her on top of my lap.

"You, you're the best love I've ever had, Vega. You're the best love I've ever had."

Our eyes locked, and there was... a longing inside of hers. For me to believe every word she'd just said. Like her life depended on me believing what she'd just said.

"I know, baby."

She closed her eyes. Her eyebrows relaxed. And she gave me a barely there smile as her eyes opened.

"Now?" I asked.

Her smile widened and she shook her head.

"Not yet."

I groaned and pulled my dick out of my boxers.

"Do you see this shit?" I wrapped her hand around my dick and she moaned. "Do you feel that?"

Jess pulled my dick between her legs and started to grind against it. She was wet as hell, and each time she moved her hips against me she put her juice on me. I started to lift her up and slide inside of her, but the pleasurable look on her face gave me enough self-control to let her do her.

"You're selfish as fuck," I mumbled gripping her waist. "Using me to get your nut while robbing me of mine."

She smiled and bit down on her lip when I pushed her down, applying more pressure to her clit.

"Vega?" She called weakly.

"Yes, baby?"

"Now."

I stood and placed her in the middle of the bed. She pulled her shirt off while I removed my boxers and slid between her legs.

The second my body hung over hers she wrapped her legs around my waist and took my face into her hands.

"You have my soul, Vega," she said softly avoiding my eyes. "You don't just... love me. You speak into my spirit. You nourish my soul. You dwell within my heart. You water and nurture the flowers in my mind. You're in every fucking part of me, nigga. *Every fucking part.*"

Her eyes returned to mine as they filled with tears. I pushed myself into her and resisted the urge to cum immediately.

"Marry me," I pleaded with my lips to hers.

"You already asked me that," she said with a smile as she ran her fingers down my ears.

"No... right now. Tomorrow. Marry me tomorrow."

Jess pulled my head up slightly to look into my eyes. She looked into them for a second... like she was trying to gauge my seriousness.

80

"This right here…" I looked down at the connection of us and so did she. "Is the only constant in my life that I know I can depend on. Us. Our union. You. I told you the first night we made love that I didn't give a fuck who you called yourself giving access to your heart to because I had every other part of you. But you have every part of me. So much so that this…"

I pulled myself out of her and slid back in deeply.

"Is the only time I truly feel whole. Like the man I'm supposed to be. When I'm connected to you. Surrounded by you. Filling you."

Her legs fell from around my waist as her walls pulsed against me. She bit down on her lip and moaned as she came. Just like that. I slid my tongue into her mouth and it swirled around hers after she composed herself. When she did I pulled myself away from her and looked into her eyes.

"I don't want nobody else to have access to what's mine inside of you. Nobody else can benefit from you the way I do. You're mine."

I lifted her a couple of inches off of the bed and pushed deeper inside of her.

"Vega," she moaned pulling me closer.

"Mine. I don't wanna wait no more. I *can't* wait no more."

"Then don't. Make me yours. Fully. Tomorrow."

"Yea?"

"Yes."

A smiled covered my face as I buried it in her neck.

"You sure?"

"Absolutely." Her fingers ran up and down my back as she kissed my shoulder.

"I love you, Vega."

"Should we tell anyone?"

"You know if we don't they will be on our asses when we go back to Memphis."

I rolled over on to my side, still inside of her, and she played with the hairs on my chin. This was the shit I lived for with her. This intimacy. This closeness. All I needed was to be inside of her and I was good.

"Fine," I mumbled running my fingers through her hair. "And I love you too."

Jess smiled and pulled herself closer to me. Her arm wrapped around me and she snuggled her head into my chest.

"Jess?"

"Yes, baby?"

"I'm hungry."

Jessica

In just a few minutes... I would be leaving the house to marry the man who irked my soul the first day we met. But even though he got under my skin... there was something about him that I was drawn to. His smile. His confidence. The way he looked at me and handled me. Like I was already his.

And now... I was about to be his for life.

I had only three more shows to tape before I was done for the season, and after that we were going on our honeymoon. Then... back to Memphis we go!

There is absolutely no doubt in my mind that this time of transition is going to be good for us. For the past four years we've been stacking our bread and chasing our dreams. Fulfilling our goals. Now... it's time for us to focus on us. On marriage. On building our family.

Our family.

Damn.

My how times change.

I watched Vega as he dressed while I sat on the edge of the bed in my undies and pumps. I wasn't putting my dress on until he was ready to leave the house. I hated sitting around in my clothes. He had to feel me staring at him because he'd looked over at me every once in a while, and smile.

"You haven't changed your mind yet?" he asked the last time he looked at me.

"Never."

My phone rang with a Facetime request from Braille. She called me yesterday but when Vega came home I completely forgot to return her or Israel's calls.

"Hey boo," I spoke when I answered.

"Hey boo! You got your dress on yet?"

"Nah. I'm still waiting for him. I'm not putting it on until we leave."

"Send me lots of pictures since y'all being stingy with the love and not having a ceremony."

I smiled and looked up at Vega. For this... he was all I needed.

"I will. He's having the guy that takes pictures at his events to meet us there so we'll have some professional ones. Jabari wants to throw us a party when we get back to Memphis so we can celebrate then."

"Great. Listen… is he around you?"

"Yea, why."

"Well… Israel has been looking for you."

"I know. I meant to call you both yesterday. What does he want?"

"Well… it's… about… Cam."

"What about him?" Vega asked as he came and sat next to me.

"I don't know exactly. Israel was just like he's been living reckless since he saw Jessie and he asked me to ask if you would call and talk to him."

I looked over at Vega, but he was looking at B.

"Tell him I'm sorry but…"

"Nah, call him," Vega interrupted.

"Why?" I asked.

"I'm secure in what I have with you. We're about to get married. It's cool. Call him."

I continued to stare at him until he pecked my lips softly.

"Call, Jess."

"Fine," I mumbled returning my attention to Braille.

"Ima let you go. I love you. Congratulations to you both. Send me those pictures!"

My smile was soft and timid as I nodded.

"I will. I love you too. See you soon."

"Bye!"

I disconnected the call and licked my lips.

"You sure?" I asked.

"Positive."

"I don't have his number."

"Get it from Israel."

Was this some kind of test? Would I fail if I called? Would I fail if I didn't? Was the test how I would react? What I would say? What he would say? With no idea what the hell to do I called Israel back.

"Hey, Jessie. How are you?"

"I'm good. How are you?"

"I'm good. Listen, I need you to rap with Cam for a second."

"Why exactly?"

"He's just... in a funk. Seeing you put him in a *what if* state. He's been thinking about how his life would have been if he would have fought harder for you. I guess seeing you happy and in your truest state did something to him."

"Oh. Well, you can give him my number and have him to call me if he needs to."

"Cool. Thank you. Normally I wouldn't say anything and I mean no disrespect to your fiancé, but I've never seen him like this before. So anything that can help..."

"I understand."

"Cool. Enjoy your day."

For the first time since I got on the phone with him I smiled.

"I most certainly will."

My eyes locked with Vega's and he smiled before leaning forward and kissing me sweetly. The phone beeped signaling Israel ended the call, but I didn't even care. All I cared about was how good Vega's lips felt against mine.

"Baby," I muttered pulling away. "Can you believe we're really about to do this?"

His smile widened.

"Damn right. You've always been mine. It's just been a matter of time."

"Cocky as usual," I mumbled as I stood.

Vega smacked my ass then pulled me down to his lap. He bit my shoulder and I moaned.

"Stop or we won't get out of here."

His reply was cut off by the ringing of my phone. Although Cameron's number wasn't saved in my phone, I recognized it immediately. I licked my lips and looked behind me to Vega.

"Answer," he ordered softly.

I nodded and answered, putting the call on speakerphone.

"Hello?"

"Jessie?"

"Hey. What's going on?"

"Shit I don't know. Just... seeing you the other day messed with me I guess."

"Why?"

"You were the you I've always wanted. I just... felt bad for not fighting for you more. Like... what if I had fought for you and not met Brittany? I just keep thinking about if we'd be together now. Doubting one decision I made is making me question every decision I've made ever since."

I had no clue what to say. I turned again and looked at Vega and he shrugged then mouthed for me to put him on hold.

"Hold on, Cam."

"Cool."

I put the call on mute.

"The hell am I supposed to say to that?" I asked.

Vega chuckled and shook his head.

"What's in your heart?"

I shrugged and shook my head.

"That I'm sorry but there was no way you would let me be with him or anyone else, so him finding Brittany was for the best."

"Okay, so maybe *don't* say that. If he was a guest on your show what would you say?"

I exhaled loudly and thought about it fully.

"That everything in life happens for a reason. If we were meant to be no time or distance would have been able to keep us apart. I mean... look at me and you, Vega. A year passed and we didn't see each other or even speak to each other. Look at us now."

"Tell him what you just said. Minus the part about us. Tell him... it's better to make the wrong decision than no decision at all. That even if it *was* the wrong decision... his life aligned with his purpose because now he's married with a child. Something he's been loving and proud of for years before he saw you. Tell him not to let the familiarity of what he has with his family rob him of his appreciation for them just because of the newness of you. Yea... tell him that."

"How am I supposed to remember all of that?"

"Just paraphrase it."

I rolled my eyes and returned to the call. Trying my hardest to remember all that Vega said. By the time Cameron and I got off the phone he seemed more at ease. He sounded like his normal secure self. That last part about familiarity really got to him. He said that's exactly what it was. That he'd gotten so comfortable with his life, that seeing me brought excitement that he hadn't experienced in a while. So, he's going to see about Brittany's parents' keeping their daughter for a week while they go on a second honeymoon.

When we got off the phone I released a heavy breath and kissed Vega on his cheek.

"How you feel?" he asked.

"I feel... like I'm ready to get out of this house to marry you."

I stood and went over to the top drawer of my dresser. After retrieving the ring I'd gotten him I walked back over to the bed, but he stood. He looked from the box to me a few times and I smiled.

"Is that... for me?"

"Yep. You want it now or when we get to the courthouse?"

"I don't know. What do you think?"

"Vega... it's your ring. Do you want it now?"

"Yea. Nah. Give it to me now. Nah. Wait until we get to the courthouse. Okay, give it to me now. Well..."

On my tip toes, I kissed him to shut his conflicted ass up. His arms wrapped around me, and I let them stay there until I pulled the ring from the box. I tossed the box on the bed and took his left hand into mine. As we kissed, I put the ring on his finger. When I was done he pulled his lips away from me... but he didn't look down.

"This makes it feel real for me," he whispered.

I smiled and kissed his hand. Kissed his finger. Kissed the ring.

"It's been no secret that I've been yours... but now... you're mine."

Hanif

After Trina, Grace's mother, went to the doctor with her, Grace was on me about putting my issues with her behind us. Really, a nigga didn't have no issue with Trina. I had an issue with the way she allowed her husband to treat her, treat Grace, and influence her to treat Grace.

I will never understand how a woman, the feminine energy, refuses to love and nurture. Especially a child. You can say you don't want a man, a relationship, love… whatever. It's a part of our design as humans to crave companionship. And just like a man needs to provide and protect to feel like a man because of his masculine energy, a woman needs to love and nurture.

So for Trina to go so against her very nature just to satisfy her husband… that bothered me. Since she was done with Bruce and had in all honesty stepped up quite a bit, I agreed to sitting down with her and trying to get past our differences.

Trina came to the coffee shop while I was opening up. It was six in the morning and she was knocking on the door like it was six in the evening. I groaned inwardly as I made my way to the door, but the closer I got to it, my demeanor softened. She was looking so… happy and at peace. Her energy immediately began to transfer to me.

And when I let her in and noticed the cake plate in her hands…

"What's this?" I asked as she handed it to me.

"A peace offering. German chocolate cake. That's your favorite… right?"

I looked at her briefly as I nodded, then headed over to the espresso machine.

"Would you like something to drink, Trina? Coffee, latte, cappuccino, tea…"

"What are you having?"

"Cinnamon latte."

"Hmmm never had one of those. I'll try that out."

As I made our drinks, she asked for a knife and plate for me to taste the cake. I told her where she could find the utensils, and I damn near ruined my steamed milk watching her cut that cake. Damn Grace for telling her German chocolate was my favorite.

I put her drink in front of her. She placed the cake in front of me. As much as I wanted to dig in, I waited until she spoke before I did. Had she said the wrong thing it would have ruined the cake for me.

"First, let me say, I admire how fiercely protective of Grace that you are. How you love her. Care for her. See to her wants and needs. She... needed that. She needed you. So... thank you."

I nodded and took a bite of the cake. My eyes closed as I savored the decadent flavors consuming my taste buds.

"It's cool," I replied after swallowing the cake and putting a bigger piece on my fork.

"I was hoping we could eventually have more than just a cordial relationship. Grace and I are getting closer. I adore Hosea. And I can't wait for Neema to get here. They're all I have, Hanif. And they're tied to you. So... can we be friends?"

"If you can make one of these cakes for every birthday I have... I think we can make that happen."

Trina smiled and nodded.

"I think I can make that happen."

"Okay... well... what about Thanksgiving and Christmas too?"

Grace

The sight before me was one I never thought I'd see. My mother seasoning meat while Hanif grilled it. Hosea was running around the backyard playing with Reign, Royalty, Power Jr. and Ellie. Power and Elle were cuddled up in the far corner of the backyard. And Rule and Camryn were playing dominoes.

Only people missing were Braille, Lorenzo, Jessica, and Vega.

But they would all be home soon.

Hanif and my mom shared a joke together and their laughs made me smile. Hanif was so at ease. He'd changed tremendously. All of the pain, hurt, and anger he'd been harboring when we met was gone. But he was still just as loving, caring, and passionate as he always was.

Just the thought of how much we'd gone through had my inner thighs leaking. I stood and made my way over to him. With my hand on the back of his shirt, I tugged gently to get his attention. He looked back and down at me and smiled.

"What's up, baby? You good?"

"Yea. C'mere for a second. I need to holla at you."

His smile widened as he wrapped his arm around me and kissed my nose.

"Wait for me in the bedroom. Let me get this meat off the grill and I'll be right up."

Lorenzo

We were in Miami for three days before the deal on the island closed. Braille still had no idea what I was up to, and I wanted to keep it that way. She hated surprises. Well, she loved surprises, but she hated not knowing what the surprise was. If I took too long to tell her what the surprise was, her excitement would wear off and she would get *so* irritated.

Shit was funny as hell.

Because she slept later than I did, I was able to leave out early enough to handle the island business and be back at the hotel by noon. When I made it back, she was eating breakfast while talking to Grace. As she talked I packed our shit up. B watched me for a second before ending her phone call.

"Hey, baby," she spoke walking over to me.

I stopped packing long enough to kiss her.

"What you doing?" She asked.

"The surprise is ready now. So I'm about to head out."

"And go where, Lorenzo?"

My smile didn't listen to me. I told it to stay in, but it was threatening to spread across my face at the tone of her voice.

"If I tell you, it won't be a surprise, Braille."

"Can I have a hint?"

"No, B. I need to go first to make sure everything is straight. Then I'm going to come back for you. If I don't make it back tonight, I'll be back early tomorrow morning."

Her eyebrows wrinkled as her mouth twisted to the side. She was trying so hard not to give me a hard time, but I could tell not knowing what I was up to was killing her. I stopped packing again, grabbed her hand, and sat her down on the bed.

"You trust me?"

"Of course, LoLo."

"Then trust me to give you the time of your life. I've been away from you for seven years. I'm making moves to make sure you realize just how much I missed you, and how blessed I am to have you. You're going to love the surprise, B. Just trust me."

I covered her neck with my hand and lifted her head slightly. She smiled as her eyes closed.

"Fine, just hurry up so you can come back to me."

"I will. Why don't you go to the hotel spa or something while I'm gone? They'll just charge it to the room so do and get whatever you want."

I pecked her lips quickly and let her go, but she grabbed my neck and pulled me back for a deeper kiss. Before I could stop myself I pushed her down on the bed and got on top of her, but I pulled myself up and returned to my bags.

I felt her watching me as I packed up the last of our things, but had I looked back, I would've ended up back in that bed with her. And for what I had planned... sex would have to wait.

Braille

Two days. It took LoLo two days to get together this surprise he had for me. For two days he came back to the hotel super late and crashed, but today... today he took me with him. First of all, I thought the boat ride was the surprise, but since we had our bags I figured we were going to be staying somewhere else for the remainder of our trip.

We get off the boat, and he told the captain that we'll be ready to go in two days. I finally looked around and realized we were on an island. A beautiful island. With palm trees, clear skies, white sand, and beautiful deep water surrounding us on all sides. It was weird because there was one lonely cottage. It looked like it was literally sitting in the middle of the ocean.

Lorenzo grabbed my hand and led me to the cottage. I squeezed his with a smile as I looked up at him.

"Where are we, baby?" I asked. My excitement growing larger and larger.

"We're... at... Braille's island. Complete privacy and seclusion. The only island for twenty miles."

I stopped walking immediately as my bag slipped from my hand. Lorenzo stopped and stood in front of me.

"Braille's island?"

His hand wrapped around my neck and he lifted my head. I looked from his lips as he slowly licked them to his eyes.

"Yes. Braille's island."

"That's a funny name. A funny coincidence," I muttered as my eyes watered and closed.

"It is no coincidence, Braille. This island... is yours. Ours. This is the surprise."

My eyes opened immediately.

"Ours? What do you mean?"

He chuckled quietly and kissed my lips softly.

"I mean... we own this shit. This is ours."

He wiped tears from my face and I shook my head.

"Lorenzo..."

"Don't start. You never let me spoil you. I just… want to show you how much I love having you in my life. I know it doesn't take me buying you things and shit to show you… but I just want to give you something you can see and feel that expresses my devotion to you. Let me. You're about to be my wife. You *are* my wife. Let your husband spoil you."

Just the sound of me being his wife… him being my husband… had me pulling my dress over my head.

"You said complete privacy and seclusion?" I asked as I unbuttoned his shorts.

"Absolutely, but you don't want to take a look around the cottage first?"

"No."

"Braille…"

"Fine," I agreed unwillingly stomping towards the cottage.

He chuckled as he grabbed the bag I dropped and my dress, but I didn't see shit funny.

The cottage had six bedrooms, a separate living and dining room, kitchen and breakfast nook, four bathrooms, and a spacious patio that I couldn't wait to lounge around on.

"This is beautiful, LoLo. I can't wait to go out to the ocean and watch the sun set. This is just… so beautiful. Thank you. You are the absolute best."

He blushed and pulled me into his arms.

"You can take off the rest of your clothes now."

Vega

I got a wife now. I'm somebody's husband. Not just somebody... but my world. My favorite girl. My backbone. My rider. My strength and my weakness. My biggest inspiration, fan, and supporter. Jessica Henderson Freeman is mine in the eyes of God and the law. I still can't believe that shit.

I guess you can't call going down to the courthouse to get married an actual wedding, but whatever it was it was beautiful. Tying ourselves to each other like that. A nigga can't even lie... I shed a couple of tears. Which made her shed a few tears. But it was all good.

Since we're only two weeks into our marriage we're still in that honeymoon phase. Fucking like rabbits. Really, that's the only thing that has changed between us. We still have the same best friend relationship. Only difference is we gets it in more. Two and three times a day. And that's probably because she finished the final episodes of her show for the season and we were able to move back to Memphis. For good. For now.

I put our house in Dallas on the market, and we've had quite a few offers to come in already, so I don't expect it to stay on the market for too long.

Monday's were always like the ultimate hustle day for us when we were back in Dallas. Most people hated Monday's but we loved them. We put in the most work on Monday because we wanted the rest of our week to be just as productive. So, today, I was meeting with Zo about what we were going to do as far as opening a business is concerned, while Jess met with a few producers here to see about starting her own production company.

As soon as I pulled up in front of Zo and B's house I couldn't help but smile. My nigga was out. His ass was engaged to his day one. And since he was clear of that probation bullshit we could smoke, party, travel, and fuck some shit up!

Braille opened the door with a smile. She gave me a hug as she normally does and I kissed her forehead.

"Where that nigga at?"

"In that damn basement. His ass be down there for hours. He's worse than Rule."

"He got it set up yet?"

"Nah. He's still working on it."

"Aight. Ima see you later then."

"Cool. What Jessie doing?"

"Meetings for the next couple of hours. She'll probably be done by dinner time, though. Maybe we all can meet up and eat somewhere. Or you or Grace can cook."

"Why Jessie can't cook?"

"You know her ass ain't gon' cook."

Braille smiled and nodded. My baby could cook, but after a long day of dealing with people she always wanted to eat out.

"Right. Well, I'm down. Just let me know."

I nodded and went down to their basement. Zo was sitting in the middle of his sectional with a blunt in one hand and a bottle of dark Jess Hypnotic in the other. I smiled and went and sat on the far right of the couch. The lights were off, so I could only see from the one lamp he had on and the TV – that was muted. Anytime this nigga zoned out like this he was up to some shit in his head.

That's probably the only reason B let him get away with shutting down for hours sometimes days at a time. Because she knew when he resurfaced it was going to be with a masterplan.

He leaned to the side to hand me the blunt and I took a quick hit before returning it.

"I've been thinking," he started. "There's plenty of clubs and lounges in Memphis. For the most part, they are all the same. We got a few classy places, but... they all end up ratchet as hell. Memphis doesn't need another club or lounge. Not when that's what everybody else is doing."

"Then what does Memphis need?"

"Something exclusive. Something expensive but worth it. Something everybody will want to be a part of, but not everyone will be able to experience. Something that will make people here step their fucking game up."

"What's on your mind?"

"A seasonal adult resort. One set up for summer, one for winter, one for spring break, and one for fall."

"Explain."

Zo leaned forward and handed me the blunt.

"We build a multimillion dollar resort. I don't expect the both of us to put up the money for it. In fact, if we're smart enough about it... we won't have to put up a dime. We can get sponsors... business owners, politicians, people who impact this city in a positive way to contribute. I was thinking the first two to start could be..."

"Power and Rule."

"Exactly. Malik and Malachi. Bishop and Rell. Israel. Khalil. Every street nigga that has gone legit needs to have a hand in this shit. When I first saw this in my head it was on a beach, but all we have here is a river. So, I was thinking we could either build near the Mississippi River, or just have pools and build our own wetland. You and Jessie... y'all are the creative ones, so I'll let you come up with what we'll offer and shit."

I nodded and handed him the blunt.

"This shit ain't gon' be easy," I mumbled more to myself than him.

"But I know it will be worth it."

I nodded again and inhaled a deep breath. I knew it would be worth it. But me and Jessie had come home to get *away* from devoting so much of ourselves to business. With us just getting married, I was looking forward to making her and making babies my priority. With an idea like this, though... I couldn't pass it up.

"Fuck it. I'm down. If this is executed properly this will be something that not only will take Memphis by storm, but the entire world. *No one* else is doing something like this. If we went global with this... we'd have a legacy that our great great great great great great grandkids will be able to live off of."

"And build on."

"Mane what."

"Aight, well, let me cut the lights on and bring some paper and shit down here so we can start brainstorming."

"Cool."

I pulled my phone from my pocket and texted Jess. She was going to have to meet me over here because this was probably going to be an all-night thing.

Jessica

I got a husband now. Like... I'm somebody's wife. Not just somebody. My boo. My best friend. My everything. My biggest headache and biggest fan. The one who sees me... flesh, flaws, and all and accepts me. Just as I am. The one who made me better. The one who helped me find me. And see myself. See past my past and the things I considered failures.

There wasn't much of an adjustment that we had to make for married life. If anything, it was just... better. It was freer. Since we've been back in Memphis and I stopped taping we've had so much more time to spend with each other. And I've been eating that shit up!

Being able to wake up without an alarm clock. And just... lay there. In my husband's arms. Make love and joke around before showering together and making him breakfast. Man... is this life? This is it. This is it.

This morning however, I ended up making breakfast for him and Hosea. I was given the chance to keep him for a few hours while Grace and Hanif looked at buildings for their third coffee shop.

I needed to talk to her soon, though. With her screenplays doing as well as they have been... I wanted her ass to write something for me! She could write and I could produce and direct. If I wanted to make the JESS network happen I was definitely going to have to get even more serious with my craft.

I don't know, though. Right now... watching Hosea sit in the middle of the floor with a bowl of Fruit Loops, that he'd picked all of the orange ones out of... this was what I wanted to focus on. My husband. Building a family with him. Not adding on another project that would pull me away from him again.

"TeTe Jessie?" Hosea called without pulling his eyes from the TV. "What's up?"

"I'm bored. You don't have nothing over here for me to do."

Hosea finally turned to look at me and I smiled immediately. This was definitely Hanif's outspoken, crazy child.

"Okay, well, what do you want to do? You want to go to Incredible Pizza or to the park or something?"

He shook his head and took another bite of his soggy cereal. I smiled as milk ran down his chin.

"Not right now. I just want you to get some stuff in your house for me to do. You don't have no kids for me to play with. No animals. Nothing. You need to have some babies for me to play with. Or a puppy. Ewww can you get a puppy?!"

Hosea jumped from the floor and came and sat next to me.

"Hosea, I am not about to get a puppy just for you to play with when you come over. You don't even come over a lot."

"Because it's boring!"

"So, you're saying... if I get a puppy you'll come around more?"

He nodded and began to swing his legs.

"What if I buy you a puppy to keep at your house and you can bring it when you come over?"

He shrugged then nodded.

"Okay, TeTe Jessie. Just hurry up and buy it because I'm going crazy!"

I laughed at his dramatic ass and mushed his head. He gave me a hug and returned to the middle of the floor. For a second... I just sat there. Deep in my thoughts. Deep in Hosea's request. Then, I grabbed my phone and went to the kitchen. I leaned against the island so I'd be able to see Hosea, but it was far enough for him to not be able to hear my conversation.

Vega answered and I smiled immediately.

"Are you *ever* going to get me pregnant... or nah?" I asked.

He was quiet for a few seconds before laughing hysterically. I mean... hysterically. And for a long time too. So long and loud I laughed myself. But I was serious.

"Yo... where that random ass question come from?"

"Hosea told me our house is boring because we don't have any kids or animals to play with."

He laughed again and I joined him willingly this time.

"That lil nigga crazy as hell, bae. I swear I love when he comes over. We need to get you pregnant so he can come around more then. But it's your fault, Jess."

"How is it my fault, Vega?"

"Aren't you on birth control?"

My straight shoulders caved in and I lost my fire. He was right. I was.

"Oh yea. I am."

"So we waiting on you. Toss them pills for me, okay?"

With a blush, I nodded as if he could see me.

"Okay."

"You mean to tell me all I had to do was get Hosea to tell my wife to have my baby and she'd listen? I would have had Christina to tell you that years ago."

"Get off my phone, Vega."

"I love you."

"I love you too. When are you coming home?"

"It'll be late, baby. Zo and I are meeting up with Power and Rule about the resort. But I'll be home in time enough to have dinner with you and shit. What you cooking?"

"What you want?"

"You know what I like."

"Okay."

I tried not to sound as disappointed as I was, but of course I couldn't hide anything from him.

"When we get this shit going it won't take as much of my time, okay?"

"Okay."

"I love you."

"I love you too."

"Bye, baby."

"Bye."

I stood there for a few seconds and tried to get myself together. But damn, I just... wanted my baby. My big baby. My Vega. Grace rang the doorbell and I quickly wiped my tears.

"Well, Hosea, looks like you can go home now," I said walking past him to the front door.

I let Grace in and shook my head at the sight of hickeys on her cheek and neck.

"Is that all y'all do?" I asked pointing to her cheek.

She blushed and covered it as we walked to the living room.

"Listen, it's not my fault that I feel loved through quality time and physical touch. We can't help it."

"Get it how you live, honey. I ain't mad at you."

"I bet you aren't. I'm going to act like I didn't hear your loud ass moaning this morning when I pulled up with Hosea."

I covered my mouth immediately.

"Oh my God. I completely forgot we had the window open this morning. Shit! I hope our neighbors didn't hear us."

Normally, I didn't get that loud. But this morning, his ass knew he was going to be gone all day and he made sure he left me well satisfied.

"Umhm. Nasty asses. Well, I gotta go. Neef is in the car and my mama wants me to stop by before we go home."

"Cool. What you doing for your birthday Friday?"

"I have no clue. Neef told me not to plan anything so I guess he has something up his sleeve."

He did. A surprise party. But I asked anyway because it would have been more suspicious of me if I hadn't than if I did.

"Alright, then. Y'all be safe. Let me know when y'all get home."

I stood and let her grab on to my forearm so she could stand up. Neema's arrival was less than two months away and I think B and I were just as excited as Grace was.

"See you later, Hosea." I kissed his forehead before grabbing his hand and lifting him up.

He took a step back and tilted his head so he could look up at me.

"Will you have the baby or the puppy by the time I come back?"

"Lawd have mercy. I know you did *not* let him talk you into getting a puppy? And what baby?"

I smiled and wrapped my arm around hers as we walked to the front door.

"It's a funny story."

Hanif

Grace turned twenty-five today. So, when she woke up... I had twenty-five bouquets of purple lilies all around our bedroom. I wasn't in the bedroom when she woke up, but I heard her the moment she opened her eyes and saw them.

She gasped, then grunted, then squealed. I smiled and shook my head as I poured my second cup of coffee for the morning. Since it was her birthday I took the day off, but I sent Hosea to daycare anyway so we could have a little time together before her surprise party tonight.

A few minutes later, Grace was walking into the den butt ass naked. Looking exotic and sexy as hell. Her glowing cinnamon skin looked smooth and shiny from the oil she'd put on it. Her belly was sticking out looking too cute. And her hair was down, flowing over and covering her breasts.

"Happy birth-"

I couldn't even get it all the way out before she was straddling me and kissing me deeply. My hands covered her cheeks and I pulled her closer to me. It doesn't matter how many times I have her... how many different ways I experience her... I *never* tire of her.

She pulled away and licked her lips.

"Thank you, Neef. Those flowers are so beautiful. Thank you."

"Anything for you."

"Where's Hosea?"

"Daycare."

"So we have the house to ourselves?"

"Yep."

"Can I have it?"

Her hips swirled around mine and I gripped her waist absently.

"Take what you want."

Grace pulled my dick from my boxers, slid down on it, and did just that.

Grace

I had no clue what Hanif was up to for my birthday, but a surprise party wasn't even the last thing on my mind. I jumped so hard when they yelled surprise that I just knew Neema was going to slide right out of me!

Those closest to me were there to celebrate my life, and the entire night was perfect. Except for the little spat between Braille, Lorenzo, and one of the cashiers at my café. Crystal is super cool and friendly. Sometimes... a little too friendly. With men.

I caught her checking Lorenzo out a few times, but I wasn't expecting her to actually make a move on him when he was clearly there with B. For the most part, they were stuck together at the hip. The only time that changed was when B and Jessie went to the bathroom together.

Crystal casually made her way over to Lorenzo. At first, Zo wasn't giving her any play. He kept looking back at the bathroom for Braille, but eventually he smiled and allowed her to flirt with him.

I saw Braille and Jessie exit the bathroom and lean against the wall as they watched Crystal and Zo talk. B's arms were folded against her chest while Jessie kept shaking her head. I tried to go over to them, but Hanif grabbed my arm and stopped me.

"Sit your pregnant ass down somewhere. You bet not go over there getting in that bullshit. It's already two of them. That's enough."

I twisted my lips and nose up at him but sat my pregnant ass deeper in my seat too. Crystal's finger caressed the beauty mark under Lorenzo's eye and I clutched Hanif's arm in disbelief. As I expected, Braille rushed over to them. I couldn't hear what she said, but she didn't say much before she hauled off and punched Crystal in her mouth.

Then she reached back to hit Zo, but he grabbed her arm, pulled it behind her back, and jumped from his seat. Jessie tried to go at him of course, but Vega grabbed her and pulled her behind him. I sighed and sat back in my seat as I watched both men practically drag my girls out while they kicked and screamed.

"Don't let that shit ruin your night, birthday girl," Hanif whispered into my ear before biting it.

A smile immediately covered my face as I caressed his cheek.

"I'm sure you're going to make sure it ends perfectly."

Hanif nodded and twisted his body in his seat.

"Ima end it just the way I started it."

My pussy throbbed just at the thought of having him inside. Happy birthday to me!

Lorenzo

Every time I thought about Braille trying to put her hands on me I looked over at her in the passenger seat and shook my head. Yea, a nigga shouldn't have let that girl be all in my face, but damn, I ain't mean no harm.

She was kind of cute and she was throwing me some attention. I didn't see nothing wrong with it. After doing seven years around nothing but niggas... a nigga liked to be reminded of how fine he was every once in a while. And Crystal had no problem letting me know she liked how I looked.

I noticed her watching me, simply because I felt somebody's eyes on me. The entire night. It wasn't nothing spectacular about her. She was a decent looking chick. Nowhere near as beautiful as my fiancée. I told Crystal about three times that Braille was my lady and she was coming back soon, but she wasn't paying me no attention.

What I wasn't expecting was for B to come at her, though. I guess because I told her that I told Crystal I was taken and she was still throwing herself at a nigga and that pissed her off. But what she wasn't gon' do was hit me knowing damn well I couldn't hit her ass back. Now that's what we weren't going to do.

The whole drive home she kept muttering under her breath and chuckling in disbelief. I started to try and talk to her, but I figured I needed to give her time to calm down a little first. By the time we made it home I opened my mouth to speak but she opened the car door quick as hell and sped walked to the front door.

I sat there for a few seconds and took some deep breaths before going inside. She was in the bedroom packing a bag. Like she was finna go somewhere.

"The hell you think you doing?" I asked walking over to her.

"Get away from me, Zo."

"So I'm Zo now? I'm just another nigga to you now?"

"That's what you acting like."

I put my hand on hers and stopped her movement. She looked to the opposite side of me and inhaled a long and deep breath before letting it go at the same time a tear fell from her eye. I knew her well enough to know that wasn't a sad tear. That was an angry tear.

"Get the fuck away from me, Lorenzo. I'm not playing with your ass."

"Why are you so mad?"

Braille jerked her hand away from me and looked at me.

"Are you serious, nigga?"

"Dead. Why are you so mad?"

"Because you had that bitch all in your face. Disrespecting me. What do you do when I'm not around? Fuck them?"

"Come on now. You know it's not that deep. I have never, nor will I ever, cheat on you."

"Just leave me alone."

"I can't do that, baby. You're my wife."

"No. I'm not. And I don't even know if I'm going to be."

"Are you serious? Because a bitch was flirting with me you don't want to marry me now?"

"Why was she all in your face, Lorenzo?" she yelled as more tears fell.

These tears… these tears were hurting tears. They weren't angry tears. She was hurting. And it was because of me.

"Braille… baby… because she liked what she saw. She was flirting with me. I wasn't flirting back."

"But you were entertaining her ass. You let her touch you. Like I wasn't even there. Do you know how embarrassing that was? The nigga that I'm supposed to be marrying lets another bitch touch all on him and stand between his legs the second I walk away. The fuck, dude?"

"I'm sorry," I mumbled trying to wipe her tears, but she smacked my hand away.

"Why? Would you do that? Why would you let *her* do that?"

I shrugged and took another step back as I put my hands in my pockets to keep from wiping her face again.

"Ion know."

"You don't know?"

I shook my head. She nodded and returned her attention to her bag.

"You're not leaving, Braille."

"Yes I am. I don't want to be anywhere near you."

"Then I'll sleep somewhere else, but you're not leaving this house."

"Then just get the fuck out."

"You're really mad? That shit didn't mean anything to me."

"But it meant *everything* to me. You wait until I've waited seven years for your ass and you propose to me to start fucking shit up. I guess you haven't had a chance to at any other time. Is this not what you want anymore?"

"This is *all* I want, B. I promise that didn't mean anything to me. I ain't gon' lie... it was nice to be flirted with. But I swear it didn't mean anything to me. I just... enjoyed the attention. It was harmless to me. And had I known it would have bothered you this much I wouldn't have even entertained her."

"So who else have you been entertaining while I haven't been around, Lorenzo?"

I guess I didn't answer quick enough because she laughed and shook her head.

"You know what... just forget it. Since my attention isn't enough... why don't you just..."

"No. Don't even go there."

"Why don't you just take..."

I closed the space between us and grabbed her neck.

"Don't."

"Let's just take a break, Lorenzo. Maybe this is moving too fast for you. I mean... you've been locked up for seven years. It's completely understandable to want to enjoy your life and freedom. I'm not trying to stand in the way of that. I'm not going to be disrespected either."

"You're trying, and failing by the way, to break up with me because I let another bitch flirt with me?"

"How would you feel if you walked up on a nigga flirting with me? Standing between my legs? Touching my face? And I'm just smiling all in his face eating up every word he's saying. How would you feel, Lorenzo?"

"It's not the same. Let a nigga get between your legs and I'm beating both of y'all asses."

"Oh... but you can flirt with other bitches?"

"I wasn't flirting with her. She was fl-"

"Flirting with you! Get out my face with that bullshit. You wanna flirt and be the center of attention you do that shit. You have my full blessing to do that shit, Lorenzo. But you gon' do it as a single man."

"Nah. Ain't no breaking up. Especially over something so petty."

"So you disrespecting me is petty?"

I released the hold I had on her and took a step back.

"I'm sorry. That wasn't my intention."

She nodded and looked towards the door.

"Can you just... go?"

"Fine. But you're not leaving me. I've waited too long to have you to lose you over something so... senseless."

Instead of saying anything, Braille started to unpack her bag. As much as I didn't want to leave with this so unresolved, her unpacking gave me enough peace of mind to let her have her space.

Braille

The hell was I doing here?

Here out of all places.

Outside of Canon's house a little after midnight.

I just… I don't know.

Lorenzo pissed me off so much. What irritated me most was the fact that he didn't see anything wrong with what he did. Like… how many other bitches has he allowed to touch on him and flirt with him? Who did he flirt back with? Has he really been faithful to me? What if he's been cheating this whole time?

My thoughts were so twisted.

And Canon was the last person I needed to be around. But he was the first person that came to my mind when I snuck out of the house. I didn't even know if he was in town or at home. All I knew was I needed to get out of that house before I strangled Lorenzo's simple, silly ass.

I twirled the ring he'd given me around a few times before pulling it off and getting out of my car. The closer I got to Canon's front door the heavier my heart felt.

The hell was I doing here?

Shit, if I wanted to get even I should have just went to Walmart and flirted with a random nigga. Went to a club and let niggas flirt with me. But Canon?

The hell was I doing here?

Not knowing the answer to that question didn't keep me from knocking on his door. A few seconds passed before I lost my nerve and started walking back to my car. The door opened and my feet stopped moving.

"B?" Canon called. "What's wrong?"

My tears started falling and I couldn't even pull myself to turn around. Canon made his way in front of me, but I couldn't look up at him. He lifted my face up by my chin.

"Are you… are you crying? The fuck is wrong with you?"

He wiped my tears, but that just made me cry harder.

"I… I shouldn't be here. I'm sorry."

I tried to walk away from him, but he grabbed my arm and pulled me into his chest.

"What is going on, Braille?"

"Nothing. I'm sorry for bothering you. I *really* shouldn't be here."

"Is everyone safe?"

"Yea... it's... nothing like that."

"So... Lorenzo fucked up?" I smiled softly and nodded. "You wanna come in and talk about it?"

"Yes, but no... I can't. Thank you. I'm so sorry."

"Okay. Well... if you change your mind. My door is always open for you."

"Your girl isn't in there is she?"

"Nah. She's at home."

"K. Goodnight."

"Goodnight, Braille."

I made my way home and sat in the car for a few hours before walking inside. Well... trying to walk inside. Lorenzo's buff body ass was standing behind the door blocking my way.

"Will you move?" I asked.

"Didn't I tell you not to leave this house? You're hardheaded as fuck, mane."

"Leave me alone, Lorenzo. I'm not talking to you right now."

"And where the fuck is your ring?" He growled yanking my hand up towards his face.

I opened my right hand and held it out for him.

"Here. I don't want it," I mumbled pushing my hand closer to him.

"Braille, I get that you're in your feelings. But if you shut down over something so petty and give me that ring back, I'm not offering it to you again."

"Are you going to take it?" I asked as tears filled my eyes.

He looked from me, to the ring, and back at me before snatching the ring from my hand and walking out of the house so quickly he damn near pushed me down in the process.

"Lorenzo, wait," I called out as my tears began to fall.

Our eyes met in the darkness.

"Make sure you wear a condom if you decide to go out and *flirt* with another bitch."

"That's the type of nigga you think I am, B?"

I shrugged and looked away from him.

"I don't know anymore."

"I'm sorry you feel that way."

"Me too."

We stood there. Avoiding each other's eyes. For so long my legs started to hurt. But neither of us made a move. I hated his ass right now, but I didn't want him to leave. And he probably could have tossed me around at this point, but he didn't want to go.

When I couldn't take it anymore I went back into the house, being sure to keep the door open for him. I made my way upstairs to our room and took a shower. After drying off and putting on some of Jessie's body butter, I put my hair up in a ball and went back into our bedroom.

He was sitting on the edge of the bed with his head down, but when I was near he lifted his head and looked at me. I took my clothes to the closet and put them in the dirty clothes basket, then climbed under the covers.

Lorenzo stood and undressed completely. When he was done he slid under the covers as well and pulled me on top of his chest.

"I'm sorry, Braille."

His hand caressed my cheek as more tears fell from my eyes.

He took my hand into his and slid the ring back on my finger.

I held my hand up and looked at it... trying not to cry even harder.

"Don't do that shit no more, LoLo. You might be able to stop me from beating your ass while you're awake. Fuck your ass up when you go to sleep."

LoLo smiled and bit down on my neck as he put me on my back.

"I promise I won't. The next female that doesn't take the hint when I tell her I'm taken... I'm mushing her ass away from me. All I need is you. The only woman I need to give me attention is you, Braille. I mean that shit. I don't want nobody else but you. I've never cheated on you or even wanted to cheat on you, and I promise I never will."

"Fine, but if you do this shit again..."

"I won't. I can't take the thought of losing you."

I ran my finger down his cheek and started to get irritated all over again.

"Have you washed your face? Let another bitch touch on..."

He shut me up with his tongue in my mouth and his finger sliding inside of me.

Vega

My baby was in her feelings. She wasn't mad or no shit like that. But she wasn't happy with the fact that for the first real month and a half of our marriage I was away a great deal of the time working on this resort with Zo. Since she was a rider she didn't give me a hard time about it, but because I knew her so well I knew she had a problem with my absence.

The first couple of weeks after our honeymoon we were together almost all day every day, but when we returned to Memphis and I started on this new project that immediately changed. We were pretty much out of the developmental phase, so my time was about to be freed up again thankfully. Now we were looking for land to build on.

I sent her to go and get her hair and nails done and she wasn't expecting me to be around today, but I had something special planned for her. When I made it up to the nail shop I texted her from outside and looked into the window to see her response.

Me: I miss my wife.

Jess looked at the message and smiled immediately. That smile quickly turned into a pout as she took a deep breath and texted me back.

Hypnotic: Your wife misses her husband. What time you coming home tonight?

I thought about my answer thoroughly before replying.

Me: Pretty late.

Which was true, since I planned on being out with her all night.

Her head flung back, she rolled her eyes, then shook her head as she texted back.

Hypnotic: Okay, baby. Be safe.

Okay baby. That's it. No... bring your ass home I'm tired of this shit. No... why can't you come home early for a change? No... Vega, you need to get your priorities straight. No... I'm tired of you being gone all the time. No attitude. Nothing that would make me feel bad, although it was clear not having me was eating her up inside.

Me: You really love me... don't you?

Jess smiled and bit down on her lip as she brushed a tear from her eye before it could fall.

Hypnotic: Duh, nigga.

I put my phone in my pocket and walked into the shop. She was so busy looking at her phone waiting for my text that she didn't look up and see who entered. When I grabbed her hand and pulled her from the massage chair she jumped until she realized it was me. Her irritation was quickly replaced with a huge smile, then her ass started crying as I pulled her into me.

"What are you doing here?" she asked into my chest.

"I wanted to see you."

Jess looked up at me and I wiped her face. I remember a time when getting her to express her emotions was like pulling teeth... and she never cried. Now, it was nothing for her to express how she felt or shed a few tears.

"I'm glad you came since you're going to have a long night."

"I'm going to have a long night with you."

She looked at me skeptically and I smiled.

"I'm taking you out tonight. So when you leave here go straight to your cousin's shop to get your hair done." I pulled my wallet from my pocket and gave her my credit card. "Stop by the mall at some point and get you a new dress. A red one. And come home as soon as you can."

I didn't think it was possible for her to get closer to me, but she did. I had to wrap my arms around her and plant my feet firmly on the ground to keep from going back.

"I can just skip the hair appointment. I'm sure you're going to mess it up tonight anyway."

I moaned within my throat before sticking my tongue out. She sucked it then connected it to hers as I grabbed a handful of her ass. Even if I wanted to hide my erection I couldn't because I had on basketball shorts. Jess looked down between us and sighed.

"I can just find something in my closet to wear too."

I laughed quietly and shook my head.

"Baby, I want you to get your hair done and buy you a new dress. Buy something sexy to go under it as well. We will have all night and tomorrow and the day after that too."

She pouted softly and wrapped her arms around me.

"You promise?"

"I promise."

"Fine."

"I'll be at home waiting for you."

"I'll be there as soon as I can."

"Cool."

I kissed her again before taking a few steps back, turning, and walking away.

∞

When Jess returned home four hours later I was deep into my nap. Her kisses woke me up. I turned from my side to my back and pulled her on top of me. As much as I wanted to dig inside of her I couldn't. The reservations I made were for a specific slot of time. So, I felt her up for a few minutes before sending her to the bathroom to get ready. I headed to the guest bathroom to get ready myself.

Her hair was still in rollers when she made it, so I wasn't sure what it was going to look like when she took them out. But when I laid eyes on her... it felt like I was looking at her for the first time all over again.

Her hair hung past her shoulders in these big, loose curls. Her makeup was fucking flawless. Natural. And it made her face look like it was glowing. But what I loved most was the red lipstick that matched her dress and shoes. The dress looked as if it was painted onto her body. It was sleeveless and it came down to her calves. Showcasing every curve in the process. The pumps she had on, though. The pumps would be the only thing she'd be wearing tonight when I had my way with her.

They were the highest I'd ever seen her wear, and the shoes themselves were red, but the heels were gold – matching her jewelry. They were thin and pointy as hell. And I knew they were doing to stab the shit out of my back when I went deep inside of her. But there was no doubt in my mind that the pain would be worth the pleasure of her.

Jess was standing there... with her hands cupped in the center of her... looking everywhere but at me... like she was shy or something.

I smiled as I walked over to her. A few seconds passed as I looked down at her before she looked up at me.

"You look amazing, baby. I really want to kiss you, but I don't want to mess your lipstick up."

"You look quite amazing yourself. It's lip stain so it won't smear."

With her permission, I licked my lips before wrapping them around hers. Her fingers grabbed my shirt immediately as she moaned. My hands cupped her cheeks, and I tilted her head for deeper access to her mouth.

"Fuck me already," she pleaded breathlessly.

"No. I worked too hard on tonight. You're going to enjoy every minute of it. And I ain't fucking you tonight. I'm making love to you."

"Vegaaa."

I kissed her to shut her up.

"Can we compromise?" she asked when I pulled away and walked over to the bed to grab my wallet and keys.

"What's the compromise, Jess?"

"You can fuck me in the beginning just for a few minutes and then make love to me for the rest of the night."

"Jess..."

"Please. You know when you do sweet shit it turns me on heavy."

"You got it backwards, baby. You be wanting to fuck when I'm sweet and loving on you, but make love when we're mad at each other."

I wrapped my arm around her waist and led her out of the room.

"That ain't backwards. That's perfect. You're showing me your love with the sweetness, so it makes me want you to get a little rough. But when I'm mad at your ass I need to feel your love."

I rolled my eyes and sighed heavily.

"Fine. I'll give you a few of the fast, deep strokes to start off."

She looked up at me and smiled while squeezing my ass. I pushed her away from me and her crazy ass just giggled.

"Don't start with that shit, Jessica."

"Whatever. You let me squeeze it while you're inside of me."

"That's the only time you can do it too. To pull me deeper inside. Any other time that shit is gay as hell."

"Mane, whatever. I can squeeze your ass if I want to."

"Aight. Keep playing with me if you want to."

"What you gon' do?"

"Ima wear that ass out tonight."

"Shit, that's what I'm talking about!"

I stopped walking momentarily and smiled as I looked at her. She stopped walking and looked back at me.

"What?" She asked with a serious face.

"I just... love your crazy ass. That's all."

Jess blushed as she grabbed my hand and pulled me closer. "I love you too."

Jessica

My baby pulled out all the stops today! First he sends me to get all dolled up. Then he surprised me at the nail shop. And for our date he rented out my most favorite restaurant downtown. The only other people there besides us were the chef and a server.

After that we went for a boat ride on the Mississippi River. Looking up into the stars as we were serenaded with a live band with his arms wrapped around me was just... just what I needed.

I would never ask him to stay home and not take care of his business. But I was getting tired of that shit. He saw Zo more than he saw me. Hell, I saw B more than I saw him. I respected their hustle, and his ambition was one of the things that made me fall in love with him... but that shit was quickly getting played out.

It was like... what's the point in having success if you don't have the time and freedom to enjoy it?

But tonight... tonight he definitely was doing a good job at making up for his absence.

When we made it back to the house, Jabari was heading out.

"The hell are you doing here?" I asked as he handed Vega his house key.

"Shit. Have fun," RiRi replied with a smile.

I stood there and watched him walk away. Scared to go in my own damn house because I didn't know what these two were up to. Vega grabbed my hand and gently pulled me towards the door. The second he opened the door I heard Marvin Gaye in the distance.

My steps slowed down as he led me to our bedroom. He looked back at me and smiled.

"What's up with you being all shy tonight?" Vega questioned.

I shrugged and looked away from him. I guess not spending as much time with him had made all of this kind of new to me. I guess I forgot how sweet he could be. How deep he could stare into my eyes. How good he could make me feel.

Instead of questioning me any further we walked the rest of the way to our bedroom in silence. He opened the door and I gasped at the sight. Our traditional lights were replaced with red light bulbs. So the room was literally filled with a red glow. Candles and incense were everywhere. Red rose petals were all over the floor and bed. Jabari's famous pink champagne cupcakes and infused strawberries were on a tray in the center of the bed along with a bottle of Cristal.

Marvin singing in the background about getting it on just pulled everything together and before I knew it I was fighting back tears. His arms wrapped around me from behind and he kissed my neck.

"Vega, this is beautiful. Thank you so much for this. All of today."

Vega turned me around to face him. He grabbed my waist and pulled me into him.

"I just wanted to do something to apologize for my absence."

"You don't have to apologize for that, baby. It's not like you were just out fucking around. You were taking care of your business."

"Yea, but, you're my top priority. I will never spend more time in the streets than I do with my wife. Even if it is for business. You come first. And I never want you to doubt that. Now take your clothes off and get on your knees in the middle of the bed."

I watched as he grabbed the tray from the bed and put it on the dresser. I didn't start undressing until he sat in his chair next to the bed and looked at me. Slowly, I peeled my clothes off and was about to kick my shoes off until he told me to keep them on. With a smile, I crawled onto the bed and got on all fours as he requested.

Percy started singing about when a man loves a woman and I looked back at Vega to find him smiling. He smacked my ass before pulling my legs apart wider.

The feel of his tongue on my clit had me locking up immediately, but he grabbed my thighs and kept my legs apart.

"You move and I'm stopping," he warned me.

I nodded and pulled my pillow close. He feasted on my pussy like it was his fucking last meal. Like I was his favorite dish. Like I was Thanksgiving dinner. His licking and sucking and moaning and fingers and fuck... it was too much...

The way he spread my lips and licked meticulously slow. The way he clamped down on my clit and applied enough pressure to make me moan. The way his finger slid in and out of me making sounds that resembled that of a chef mixing a dish of thick and creamy consistency.

It was too much.

By the time Barry was singing about her being the one he needed I was coming and falling into the bed. I struggled to regain my breath as Vega undressed. Staring at me the whole time. When he was done he grabbed my ankle, turned me over to my back, and pulled me to the edge of the bed.

He stood there and stared at me until the song changed. When Kevin Gates *Pourin' the Syrup* started playing I couldn't help but laugh at his silly ass.

"You want me to fuck you, right?" He asked as he put my ankles on his shoulders.

"Please," I mumbled grabbing my breasts.

Vega slid into me with one smooth deep stroke. My legs weakened slightly, but when he lifted my ass off of the bed I was able to keep them steady. He pulled himself out of me and dove back in hard. Fast. Deep. So deep I couldn't even moan. All I could do was open my mouth and gasp for air.

His strokes continued. Just as fast. Just as deep. Just as hard. So consistent. Skin against skin. So loud. So fucking good. My walls started tightening around him and he groaned as I came.

His grip on my left leg loosened and it fell. Vega wrapped it around his waist and held the right one in the air. Opening me wider. Stroking me deeper.

"Fuck me back," he mumbled speeding up.

I shook my head no and fought my orgasm. Had I moved and added that extra friction I would be coming again. And by the third orgasm I would be too weak and overwhelmed.

"You not gon' fuck me back?"

His smile scared me. If I didn't do it willingly he was going to put me in a position that would force me to unwillingly.

I started lifting my hips to meet his strokes and I regretted it immediately. I was moaning and coming by the fifth one.

"Okay. Make love to me now," I pleaded.

Vega released me and I moved to the center of the bed.

"Get on your knees."

"Noooo," I whined.

Like this wasn't my bright idea. Like I hadn't asked to be fucked.

"Come on. You got one more fuck song to go."

"Don't make me cum."

He nodded with his lying ass, but I got on my knees anyway.

I arched my back, but he held my shoulders down and I knew he was about to do just what he said he was going to do... wear my ass out!

Diego by Tory Lanez came on and I mumbled *shit* under my breath. If he had much of a hype song... this was it.

Instead of getting on his knees behind me he squatted and slid down and so deep inside of me it felt like he was about to go from my pussy to my stomach. From this angle he was hitting my g-spot each time he dug inside of me and I was grunting and moaning *fuck* over and over and over as I tried to remove myself from his grip.

God, it hurt so bad that it felt so good. Felt so good it was scary to know a person could have this much control over you. A person could make you feel so good. So out of yourself.

"Stop fighting it and take it," he commanded quietly.

He slowed down just a little and I stopped my fighting. My fists gripped the sheets. My teeth bit down on my lip. My eyes squeezed shut tightly. My walls latched on to him and he moaned as he pulled out.

"It's so wet and deep and hot. I can literally feel your heat, baby," he observed before sliding back into me.

I couldn't speak. All I could do was enjoy the feel of him inside of me. And in no time I was coming yet again. This time when I fell into the bed I had no plans of getting back up. Vega turned me around to my back and tried to wrap my legs around his waist, but they fell immediately like limp noodles.

He chuckled as he laid them flat on the bed and slid back inside of me.

"Shit," he moaned as he put half of his weight on my body.

We were chest to chest. Neck to neck. His forehead was on mine as he looked into my eyes. In this position he would be coming in no time because it allowed him to feel me even tighter and deeper. But it would also be torturous for me because he would be hitting my spot each time he filled me.

Al Green's *Love Sermon* came on and Vega began to slowly move in and out of me. His eyes closed. His lips opened. His hands pulled my hair.

I licked and sucked his neck until he moaned and tried to pull himself up, but I found the strength to wrap my legs around him and keep him close.

His strokes became less consistent. Less coordinated. Quicker. Choppy. He groaned and buried his head in my neck.

"I love you, baby," I whispered as I wrapped my arms around him.

"Fuck, Jess. I... love you too," he groaned as he came inside of me.

My legs fell again and he put the entire weight of his body on me as he inhaled and exhaled deeply.

I circled my hand around his back until his breathing normalized. Shortly after he was snoring. He only did that when he was super tired. I pulled myself from under him as carefully as I could but as hard as he was sleeping I didn't imagine him waking up any time soon.

I wiped myself off and pulled my hair up, then I went into the bedroom and tried to put his heavy ass on his back so I could wipe him off. When I did I blew all of the candles and incense out. I grabbed the champagne and went out of the room and down the hall a little to open it to keep from waking him.

When I returned I grabbed a cupcake and went back to the bed. Sitting up against the headboard, I took a few sips of the champagne before biting into my cupcake.

"Gimme some," he mumbled sliding up and putting his head in my lap.

"I thought you were sleep?"

I put the cupcake down to his mouth and he took a bite.

"That towel woke me up."

"Well, go back to sleep, baby. You seem tired."

"I am, but this is our special night."

After putting the cupcake down, I cupped his cheek in the palm of my hand and lifted his head. When our eyes met I shook my head at how sleepy he looked.

"Every night I spend with you is special. Rest, baby."

Vega nodded and pulled me down further on the bed.

"Boy, you about to make me waste this champagne."

He didn't respond. He just laid his head between my breasts and wrapped his arms around my waist. His heavy ass leg covered both of mine and I smiled. I took one last sip of the champagne before putting it on the bedside table so I could eat my cupcake with one hand and rub his back with the other.

Lorenzo

There had been some slight static between B and I since Grace's birthday party. She was trying to act like she was over the whole Crystal thing, but I could tell she was having a hard time trusting me. Whenever I would go out to work on this resort shit with Vega she'd looked sad. Like she felt like I was up to some shit and didn't really want me to go.

She would never say that, though. Nor would she question me or tell me that she didn't trust me. She just... held that shit in and let me do what I had to do. I hated that her trust in me had wavered, but there was really nothing more that I could do besides love on her as hard as I could and let time and my actions show her that she was the only one I wanted.

Since we were done with the developmental phase and now looking for land to build on, I had a lot more time on my hands, so I wanted to do something special for Braille. Really, I wanted to take her back to the island, but she was working again so we couldn't make that trip just yet.

But I was determined to do something here in Memphis that would be just as special. She hated for me to spend money on her. She would rather stay in than go out. And she prefers small gestures of love and loyalty over extravagant, public displays.

So I thought and thought about what I could do that wouldn't cost hardly any money, inside the house, that would be fun and show her just how much I love and want her. Something sweet, simple, and thoughtful.

Then it hit me. I knew exactly what to do.

Today, she had to work a fourteen-hour shift instead of twelve. The minute I laid eyes on her I could tell she was completely drained of her energy, but that didn't stop her from asking me if I needed her to fix me something to eat. I led her to our bedroom and sat her on the bed. After pulling her shoes and clothes off, I ran her a bath and carried her inside.

She sat in there for so long I thought she fell asleep, but when she did come out she looked refreshed. Braille walked over to me and stood in front of me. Her hands ran down my cheeks before she leaned down and kissed me. Just a peck. A quick, soft peck. And I sighed. She was still closed off. Normally I had to keep her from sticking her tongue into my mouth if we weren't about to have sex, lately she hadn't even been trying.

I stood and removed her towel. Picked her up. Laid her on the bed on her stomach. I greased her scalp and brushed her hair until she fell asleep, then I woke her up with a full body massage. After that, I kissed damn near every part of her body that I could see. Not in a sexual way, but in a sensual, appreciative way. By the time I was done I could literally smell her pheromones secreting.

Her eyes were low. Her mouth was partially open. Her breathing was ragged. And her cream was puddling up right at her opening. I didn't want to have sex with her, though. I mean I wanted to, but I didn't want her to think that's what I was up to.

"How you feeling?" I asked as I pulled a stack of takeout menus from the drawer of our bedside table.

"Like I want my future husband to make love to me."

I looked back at her quickly and watched a slow smile spread across her face.

"B... I didn't... I just... wanted to..."

"I know what you were trying to do, LoLo, and I appreciate and love you for it. I definitely needed it."

I nodded as I sat the menus on the table.

"Now... I need you inside of me."

"Are you sure?"

We hadn't had sex since that night, and I was honestly afraid that that would make the way she felt worse. I hardly had time to really spend with her. I didn't want her thinking I wanted to spend the little time I did have fucking.

"I'm positive. Unless you don't want to?"

"Girl, please. Of course I want to."

I stood and removed my clothing, then made my way between her legs. I ran my fingers down her cheek and stared into her eyes.

"B... you know I love you."

I meant it as a question, but when it came out...

"I know you do."

"Do you trust me?"

"I wouldn't be here if I didn't."

"I don't want us going into our marriage so distant. I want... I *need* my baby girl back. What do I have to do to get us back to that space, Braille?"

"Just be with me. Just be with me."

I nodded, then lowered my head to kiss her. Her hands wrapped around my neck as I slid my tongue inside of her mouth. She lifted her hips and the feel of her wetness against me almost made me nut. I pulled myself away to focus on her bottom set of lips.

Once I had her lips spread wide, I used the tip of my tongue to tease the top of her clit. She was moaning and trembling with little to no contact, and when I sucked on that clit she was trying her best to push me away. There was a spot, right at the bottom of her lips, that with the right amount of pressure would have her coming hard. I started circling my pointing finger there as I continued my assault on her clit.

"LoLooo, stoooop," she pleaded.

Like I would listen. That only made me lick faster, suck harder, and finger her slower. Then it hit me... I was still the only man she'd ever shared her body with. I stopped immediately and looked up at her.

"What's wrong?" she asked sitting up.

I lowered my head and shook it. My body covered hers again and I felt bad as fuck for ever putting her in the mental space to even think she wasn't enough. She was *more* than enough. Loving, down, and loyal as fuck.

"I'm just so sorry, Braille."

She chuckled and wrapped her legs around me.

"Lorenzo, stop apologizing. We're good."

"Are you sure? I just feel so bad. You been down for a nigga and..."

"I didn't let seven years of jail time pull you away from me. Do you really think I'm going to let a bitch damage us? I've invested too much into this to give it away so foolishly. Besides... I want our baby to grow up with both parents in the home."

I can't imagine how crazy I was looking, but however I was looking it made her laugh. She wrapped her arms around my neck and bit down on her lip. My hand massaged her stomach and she shifted under me with her eyes closed like that was the most pleasurable thing I'd ever done to her.

"My baby... you're... Braille... you're... our baby?"

She laughed again at my failure of asking a complete question and I didn't even care.

"Are you trying to ask me if I'm pregnant?"

I nodded and closed my mouth to keep from dripping slob on her.

"Yes, Lorenzo. I'm pregnant."

I inhaled a deep breath before jumping up from the bed and grabbing my clothes.

"Lorenzo... what are you..."

I quickly went back over to the bed, grabbed her by the back of her head, and kissed her until she pushed me away.

"Thank you so much, B. Thank you for carrying my seed. Thank you for never giving up on me. Thank you for marrying me. We... we gotta get married soon. Soon."

She watched me as I hurriedly put my clothes back on.

"Lorenzo... where the hell are you going? What are you doing?"

"We need to go shopping."

"Shopping?"

She looked at the clock on the dresser then back at me.

"It's nine o'clock at night. Where are you going to go shopping?"

"Shit, I don't know. Walmart. Here..." I went into her drawers and pulled out some shorts and a tank top. "Put this on so we can go."

"Lorenzo, what are we shopping for?"

"The baby. Stuff for the baby."

"Lorenzo, we don't even know what we're having yet."

"We can just get gender neutral shit. Or like... a bed... and a bike."

"A bike? Nigga, the baby won't be able to ride a bike for years. Come sit your hyper ass on this bed."

I felt my lips poking out as my eyebrows wrinkled, but she raised hers and tilted her head to the side so I drug my feet back to the bed and sat down next to her.

"I'm happy that you're excited..."

"Excited? I'm... I'm... I don't even know a word to describe how I feel right now, Braille."

She smiled and covered her hand with mine.

"But you can't leave this house in the middle of the night after you've made my pussy wet. If you want to go and *maybe* look at some things tomorrow we can, but we're going to be sensible, okay?"

"Mane..." I mumbled the rest under my breath inaudibly so she wouldn't hear me.

"LoLo, I'm serious."

"Alright, alright. I'll... be... sensible with the spending. Tomorrow."

Braille rolled her eyes and hugged me. I pulled her on top of me and held her close.

"Thank you, baby. For real. Say, why don't we make tomorrow a day of planning for our future? Let's plan for this baby and our wedding. We already know where we're going to have it and who we're going to invite. Let's get this shit together."

She chuckled against me but it turned into a moan when I squeezed her ass.

"Baby, I don't need much. Just you and a Minister. And those closest to us."

"So, if I could put all of that together by this weekend you'd marry me?"

B pulled herself from my chest and looked into my eyes.

"You mean it?"

I nodded before pecking her lips. She didn't pull away. She connected her fingers behind my head and pulled my lips back to hers. I smiled. My baby was back. And now... she was about to have our baby.

Braille

I didn't plan on telling Lorenzo that I was pregnant in that manner. When I found out a week ago I started coming up with cute ways to tell him, but last night... it just felt right. He'd been feeling guilty as hell about that stunt he pulled when we were at Grace's party. I know my energy was probably off, but now that I think about it... it was probably just my hormones having me overly emotional.

There was no way in hell I was going to let one night of flirting rob me of my future with Lorenzo. I'd waited too long and endured too much to let it go so easily. Now, I wasn't going to sit around and allow him to cheat and disrespect me, but you better believe his ass was going to have to deal with my crazy ass and Rule and Power before he was able to get rid of me.

Last night, though. Last night felt like we got back to us. The old us. The carefree us. The loving us. And we desperately needed to get back to that. Sure enough, when I woke up, he was sitting on the edge of the bed watching me. Waiting for me to wake up. I looked at him briefly before closing my eyes and turning my back to him.

Did he catch my drift? Nope. He just sat there until I woke up again. This time he didn't let me go back to sleep. This time he picked me up and carried me to the bathroom and forced me to get ready. And when I say forced me... I mean forced me. After I unwillingly showered and shit I dressed and fixed us a light breakfast.

Then we were off to Walmart. Then Target. Then Babies R Us. Then Carters. Then a whole bunch of other baby stores. By the time we came back home I was just as tired as I would have been had I worked a full shift at the hospital! But I couldn't rest. Noooo... he bought six pregnancy tests just to be able to see the positive signs since my doctor's appointment was another week away.

And then, he invited everyone over to celebrate.

As tired as I was by the end of the night I went to sleep with a smile knowing he was the happiest he'd ever been in his life because of the seed... his seed... that was growing inside of me.

Vega

You don't really realize how far you've come until you're about to enter a new stage in your life. A different level. That's exactly how I felt as I watched Zo flip through tuxedos for his wedding.

We went from these lil street niggas to business men. Men with wives and him with a kid on the way. His ass was on ten earlier this week when B told him that she was pregnant. That nigga had everybody over celebrating like they had just won a billion dollars. But I guess when you value something and you finally get it that's exactly how it feels.

I was happy for my nigga, though. Happy that he was finally free and able to do as he pleased. Happy that he got his woman. Just... happy. Love will do that to you. I find myself randomly smiling and shit now because of all of the love that I have in my heart.

Love for and from Jess.

"Your pops called me this morning," he informed me.

"For real? What he talking about?"

Zo shrugged and sat down.

"Just was like he heard I was getting married and had a kid on the way. Told me to swing through so we can rap about some shit."

When Lorenzo's pops died my pops kind of stepped up. Not so much to take his place, but to be that male figure he was missing out on. So it didn't surprise me that he reached out to Zo.

"That's what's up. When you going?"

"Shit Ion know. It'll have to be today or tomorrow since we're leaving for the wedding Saturday."

"How you feel about that shit? Does it seem real to you yet?"

He smiled and shook his head.

"Man... nah not really. Like... she's always been mine, you know? And I always felt like if any woman would have my kids it would be her. Even if I got out and she was with somebody else I was going to find a way to trap her ass. But now... now that it's really happening... I can't believe it."

He stood and looked at me before pulling a tux from the rack and asking...

"What's it like?"

"What?"

"Marriage."

"Shit, I ain't deep enough in it to answer that. Ask Hanif. All I know is… since we exchanged those vows… it's like… everything is magnified."

"Explain."

I sat back and really thought about how I could explain this shit in a way he could understand it.

"It's like… the way we connect is deeper. Our friendship is deeper. Our love is deeper. Our loyalty is deeper. Our understanding is deeper. Our compassion is deeper. The sex is fucking… unbelievable. I guess there's a security that marriage provides versus when you're just dating someone. It allows you to experience each other on a deeper level. We're more open and trusting with each other. I don't know. It's like… it's just better. It's just deeper. We're just closer."

"Sounds like it's worth it."

"It is. It is. If I could have married her the day I met her… I would've."

Zo nodded and put the tux back.

"The fuck am I wearing a tux on an island for?"

I shrugged and ran my hand down my face.

"Ion know. I ain't."

"Mane, she just gon' have to let me wear some shorts and a button down."

I laughed… only because I knew he was serious. And Braille was not going to have that shit.

Jessica

We were dress shopping, and I was trying hard as hell to not be a party pooper, but I woke up feeling like shit. Really, I had been feeling like this for the past couple of days. My breasts were sore as hell. I was super tired. Bloated. And nauseous. I thought maybe I'd had too much champagne and cupcakes a couple of nights ago... but I had less than a cup... only a few sips... and well... maybe four cupcakes. But that's about how many I always eat and I never have any issues afterwards.

This was the first day I'd actually vomited, and that's when it hit me... I got off of my birth control a month ago. And I *could* very well be pregnant. Since I wasn't sure I hadn't said anything to anyone about it. Not even Vega.

But I was about to have to since the sales associate that was helping us was offering me a glass of wine. Both Braille and Grace declined, and now she was standing in front of me with a tray full of wine, cheese, and fruit.

"Umm... no thanks," I mumbled softly avoiding Grace and B's eyes.

"No thanks?" B repeated.

"Water is fine."

"Water is fine?" she repeated.

"Are you going to repeat everything I say?"

"Everything you say?"

I cut my eyes at her and she laughed.

"I'm just messing with you, Jessie. Since when do you turn down a glass of wine?"

I shrugged and waited for the associate to walk away.

"Since I've been feeling like crap. Since I woke up with morning sickness."

They both grabbed my wrists since I was sitting in between them.

"Oh my God! Are you... do you think you're pregnant?" Grace asked.

I shrugged again.

"That would be perfect!! Our kids will be around the same age! Neema will be just a little older... and Hosea will be the big bro that keeps everybody in line! With his mean ass!"

"Don't be talking about my baby!" Grace yelled with a smile.

She knew he was just like his daddy.

"Whatever, when are you taking a test?" Braille asked.

"I don't know. I guess today."

"Come on. Let's go to my house. LoLo bought six but I only took two."

She stood and grabbed my hand.

"Wait... we have to finish..."

"Girl, fuck these dresses. We weren't going to find anything in here anyway!"

∞

I was a nervous wreck. The test had been sitting on the counter in the bathroom but I was too nervous to get up and look. I just sat there. On the floor. Across from the bathroom. Rocking. I mean... this was what we wanted, so why was I so scared? I guess because it felt like shit was about to get real.

What if he leaves like my pops did? No, he would never do that. He's not a runner. He's a fighter. What if I suck as a mother? What if I drop it? Why am I calling it an it? I just called it an it again.

"Fuck!" I yelled leaning my head against the wall.

"What's wrong?" Grace asked wobbling over to me.

I shook my head and pulled my knees to my chest.

"Nothing. Just thinking. What were we thinking, Grace? A baby? Us?"

My tears started falling and I covered my face.

"Braille! Come get on this floor with this girl. If I get down there I won't be able to get up."

Grace ran her hand through my hair to console me and that just made me cry even harder. She was a mother. A nurturer. It was in her blood. She's always been this way. Me on the other hand? Not so much.

Braille came and sat next to me and pulled me into her side.

"What's wrong, Jessie?"

"I can't be nobody's mama. I don't know anything about being a mama. Me and Vega will screw this child up."

"No you will not. I don't know anything either. We're going to learn together. From our mother's. From Grace. From Camryn and Elle. We got this, boo. Have you even looked at the test yet?"

"No. I was too scared."

"You want me to look?" Grace asked.

"Yes, please. Don't tell me."

"Don't tell you?"

I shook my head no and buried it in Braille's neck.

"So… what you want me to do?"

"Just… I don't know. Just look first."

A few seconds passed and when I felt like she should have made it to the bathroom and looked I pulled my head up and looked into the bathroom. Grace was standing over the sink looking down at the test.

"Well… do you want to know?" she asked looking at me.

"Yes. What does it say? Am I pregnant?"

She giggled in true Grace fashion and nodded.

"Yes, mama. You're pregnant."

If my heart could have propelled me into the wall it would have. That's how heavy it felt.

"Wow. Okay. Um. Cool."

I stood. So did Braille. We stood there. Them looking at me. Me looking at the test. And then… it hit me. And I smiled. And I cried. But this time when I cried… they were happy tears. Braille took me into her arms. Grace joined us. And all of our asses were crying then.

Lorenzo

The night before we all left for the island, the niggas got together at Rule's crib and the ladies got together with Elle at Power's crib.

We ended up going to the casino in Tunica and not getting back until five in the morning, and even though I'd been up all night I still wasn't sleepy. Nerves I guess.

They were knocked out all over the house. Vega got so wasted his ass literally dropped in the middle of the hallway. Power was stretched across the couch in the living room. Hanif's big ass was sleeping sitting up in a chair. And Canon was sleeping on the dining room table.

The only person I didn't see was Rule. I figured he'd made it to his bed, but when I stepped in after smoking my third blunt I saw him going to the kitchen.

· I made my way to one of their guest rooms, but he stuck his head inside of the door and motioned for me to come with him. We went into his man cave as usual.

This was what I'd been dreading. The *you marrying my sister and if you don't do right by her and y'all kids I'll kill you* talk. I didn't even have a hard time with her father when I told him we were getting married. He said… I'll let Rule handle that. So I knew it was about to be some shit.

We sat across from each other and he lit up another blunt, but I was already half faded so I declined it.

After he took a puff he started talking.

"The first day I met Braille I knew she was special. She was wild and carefree like Camryn. Guarded like Camryn. Fiesty and stubborn like Camryn. Even though they hadn't grown up together, they had so much in common that when they did start hanging out their relationship bloomed quickly and naturally.

Because their father is white I always felt like I had to step up a little more as Braille's brother. Not that Edward is weak or anything like that. But… I needed to be sure that Braille had a strong male presence in her life so she'd choose her husband wisely. And I needed to be sure that whatever man she gave herself to knew he wouldn't get away with treating her like anything less than the Queen she is.

I remember the day you got locked up. She literally cried all day. Made herself sick. She was so fucked up over you. And that shit pissed me off. I wanted to find your ass and handle you I ain't gon' lie because she was heartbroken, but I realized... it affected her so much because she loved you so much.

She mourned your absence like you were dead. And I promised her that I would keep her from ever having to feel that way about a man again. But I didn't have to go into protector mode because you stepped up. Even though you couldn't be there for her physically you tried to be there for her financially. And you had Canon watching over her. Then... when you were ready... you stepped back into her life emotionally and mentally.

It was then that I stopped seeing you as a young nigga that was trying to take my little sister, but I saw you as a man that was trying to build with and be with his woman.

Women like Camryn and Braille... they don't come around often. So when you're blessed to be with them... you give them your all because they deserve it. Can I trust you to do that?"

"No doubt. I honestly wouldn't be here if that's not what I planned on doing. Braille is a damn good woman and I know she deserves someone far better than me, but because she chose me I'm dedicated to spending the rest of my life showing her that she made the right choice."

"And you're done with the streets?"

"Absolutely. I'm not doing anything to jeopardize my freedom. I'm not doing anything that will pull me away from her and my seed. And that includes fucking off with somebody else."

He nodded and leaned back in his seat.

"You know if you don't do right by them..."

"I know I know... you'll kill me."

Rule smiled and stood. I stood. He extended his hand for me to shake. I took it and it turned into a hug.

"Welcome to the family, Zo. Welcome to the family."

Braille

I'd gotten so used to sleeping with Lorenzo that spending the night away from him felt awkward. Grace, Jessie, Camryn, and I met at Power and Elle's house. To prepare for the wedding we all got manicures and pedicures. Our hair done. Massages. And Cam and Elle took a few shots just to rub in the fact that they were done having kids for the moment and the three musketeers all ended up pregnant at the same time somehow.

I still can't really put together how I got to this point. Like... okay... I had a flat tire seven years ago that leads to me meeting the sweetest no nonsense selfless fine man that would literally change my life.

And become such a huge part of it.

Just the thought of it brings tears to my eyes.

Most people couldn't understand my loyalty to him. How I waited seven fucking years for this nigga. But what they don't understand is that I literally had no choice. Like... my heart belongs to Lorenzo Bush. It held love for him and him alone. No other man could have access to it. Giving up on him would have been the equivalent of me giving up on love. My love. My heart. My future. Marriage. Babies. Because he encompasses all of that for me.

We may have had a brief rough patch, but being that that was the only one bad thing I could think of that he did... besides calling himself ignoring me for damn near three years... our good far outweighed the bad. And I was looking forward to spending the rest of my good days with him.

I looked around me at my girls. My sisters. All married. And I was just hours away from joining their club. I wasn't sure how this would work out. How good at it I would be. But there was no doubt in my mind that it would be worth it.

LoLo and the rest of the boys were obviously having a blast because he sent me a video of them at the casino. I wanted to go! But we agreed we wouldn't see each other until we made it to the island tomorrow. Who said we couldn't text though? I stood and went into the guest room I was staying in, got in the middle of the bed, and texted him.

Me: LoLo.

Baby daddy: I love you.

Me: I love you. Looks like y'all are having fun.

Baby daddy: Yea, it's lit. I'd rather be with you, though.

Me: Stop lying.

Baby daddy: Haha whatever, girl. You miss me?

Me: I do. How am I going to sleep without you tonight?

Baby daddy: Check your bag. I put something in there for you.

Excitement bubbled over in me as I dropped my phone on the bed and walked over to my bag. I opened it and smiled at the sight of a teddy bear with a note attached to it. When I brought it up to my nose I inhaled Lorenzo's cologne.

He was always doing simple, sweet, and thoughtful shit like this. And I swear this was all I needed! I took my happy self back to the bed and read the note.

Braille,

Feels like my old jail days, huh? Writing you letters and shit. I figured you would be missing a nigga while we were apart so I just wanted to give you something you could hold. Something you could feel. I know it doesn't compare to the real thing… but I hope it can get you through the night. Don't get too comfortable with that bear, though, because when we get back home he will not be in bed with us.

I know I've said this before… but thank you, baby. Thank you for not giving up on me. For opening your heart back to me after I left you. For saying yes. For nurturing my seed. Thank you for you.

I love you, and I can't wait to start this new phase of our lives together. It probably won't be easy, and I know I may fuck up sometimes and get on your nerves… but I love you, girl. And we in this shit together. Rub on your stomach for me and tell my little princess daddy will be around to kiss her soon.

I love you,
Lorenzo

After wiping my face, I grabbed my phone and texted him back.

Me: Thank you so much, LoLo. This was exactly what I needed. It was perfect. You're perfect. Perfect for me.

Baby daddy: Get some sleep, baby. I love you. So much. I can't wait to make you mine.

Me: Me either. I love you too. Goodnight.

And with that I snuggled up under the covers with my teddy bear and let sleep find me.

Vega

The second we made it to the island I had one mission – finding my wife! This was the first night we'd spent apart... shit... in years. When we traveled we traveled together. Even when we were mad at each other we still told each other we loved each other and slept together at night.

In fact, the only time we hadn't slept together was that night in Memphis. I ain't even plan on doing that shit. I was just so tired I couldn't make it to the bed. I expected her to come and crawl under me if she saw me, but she just covered a nigga up and gave me my space.

So I was miserable without my baby. I drunk to numb it, but I just ended up fucking my own self up with that.

She was here. She was close. I was catching her scent in the wind. Chocolate. Coconut oil. Cocoa butter. I made my way into the cottage and looked in every room until I found her. She was laying on her back with her hands cupped together on her stomach.

I closed and locked the door and made my way over to the bed. Jess looked at me as I took my shoes and pants off with a small smile. I got in the bed next to her and she laid on my chest instantly.

"I missed you," I muttered into her hair before kissing her forehead.

"I missed you too. Why did you get sloppy drunk last night?"

I shrugged as she ran her hand down my chest.

"Cause I missed you."

Jess lifted her head and looked at me with a smile.

"Vega?"

"What up?"

"Um, I should probably tell you something."

"What?"

She sat up and I did the same. Her feet were on the carpeted floor. Her palms were on the bed on each side of her. Her head was lowered. And I was starting to get a little anxious. Had she fucked off on me?

"You knocked me up."

Her eyes met mine hesitantly. My mouth opened and closed and I shook my head.

"I did what?"

"I'm pregnant, Vega."

Jess grabbed my hand and caressed it with her thumb.

"Say something," she urged.

I couldn't. I opened my mouth… but nothing would come out. She smiled and her eyes watered.

"What's wrong?" I asked.

"You're crying."

"No I'm not."

"Yes you are, Vega."

She wiped my face and I felt the wetness. I patted my cheeks when she removed her hand. Damn. I *was* crying.

"Does that mean you're happy?"

"Damn right!" I yelled pulling her face and lips to mine. "I got a lil nigga in here?"

I placed my hand on her stomach and she nodded.

"Maybe. Or… it's a little girl."

"Hell nah. I'm not trying to have to deal with another you. I need some testosterone in the house."

"Whatever," she spoke softly with a pout.

I stood and paced briefly. Me? A father? Was I really ready for this? I mean… we wanted this, but now that's it's reality…

"You trust me to not fuck this up, Jess?"

She stood and stopped me from pacing by grabbing my forearm and pulling me towards her. Her arms wrapped around my neck. Mine wrapped around her waist.

"I had a mini meltdown myself the day I took the test, but I know we can do this, baby. We have so much love and wisdom around us that we can feed off of. We're already set up to take care of her…"

"Him…"

"Her or him financially. Because we made those moves we have the time to really invest in her…"

"Him…"

"Her or him. I didn't grow up with my father, and I know firsthand that nothing compares to that presence. That love. That guidance. That acceptance. And I know you will be able to give that to our baby. You're loving. And fun. And wise. And giving. And selfless. And patient. But you're firm and you take no shit or disrespect. We got this. *You* got this."

I kissed her again before falling to my knees before her and kissing her stomach until she moaned and pushed me away.

"I don't know why that's turning me on... but seeing as the wedding is two hours away we don't need to take it there."

"Why not? I can get my nut in three minutes."

Jessica

Lorenzo's mom and sisters and Braille's parents made it for the wedding this morning. There was so much nervous, happy energy in their cottage. So much love. So much peace. So much unity. Zo and B hadn't seen each other for a day and a half now, and my girl was ready.

The ceremony was small, with only close family attending. There was no band. We were all facing the ocean, but when Camryn began to sing 'Flaws' by Kierra Sheard, we all turned towards the cottage and saw Braille looking absolutely stunning next to her father.

Sometimes I talk a lil too much, don't listen enough. Sometimes it's way too easy for me to beat myself up. Sometimes I hate the way I look when I look in the mirror. One look from you I know. My flaws…

Her dress was a strapless corset, with a v neck dip. It had a wrap style skirt with a wide thigh high split. Instead of wearing traditional shoes she had on a pair of barefoot sandals. With large curls framing her face, and glowing makeup, Braille looked like a goddess.

You love you love my flaws. Think they make me beautiful. You don't see them as flaws at all. That's why, that's why I love you. Cause you are you are the one who. The one who loves my flaws.

I pulled my eyes away from her briefly to look at Zo, and his big, tough ass was avoiding her. He had literally turned to the side to avoid seeing her. Tears immediately filled my eyes. Braille hung her head and shook it.

Vega and Rule were on both sides of Zo whispering something to him that I couldn't hear. He shook his head no and wiped the tears from his eyes. Then finally, he turned, and faced his bride.

Braille smiled and lowered her head again.

Sometimes I get a little unsure, a lot insecure. Sometimes I know I might say some words that might cause some hurt. Sometimes I get in my own way. I'm way too much to put up with. But you put up with it all - my flaws.

Lorenzo covered his mouth and shook his head as tears fell from his eyes. As if he couldn't believe she was his. That he was finally marrying her.

When she made her way in front of him, they both wiped the tears from each other's faces. Vega looked back at me and winked, causing me to blush.

Who would have guessed a flat tire would have led to Braille meeting Lorenzo? And a trip to the mall with Braille for a present for Grace would have led to me meeting Vega.

Now, we're all married, working towards families and legacies to leave behind for them.

I can't lie… most of my life… my heart had been on reserve. And I had absolutely no plans of letting any man completely in. But the right love from the right man will quickly have you rethinking things you never thought were possible.

Epilogue

Grace and Hanif

I was tired. I should have been sleep. But I couldn't resist watching the two most important men in my life – Hanif and Hosea – get acquainted with the newest member of our family. Neema. She was only a few hours old, and she had already stolen both of their hearts. The second Hosea laid eyes on Neema he kissed her forehead and told her he loved her.

I can only recall seeing my husband shed tears four times. As he grieved for his brother. On our wedding day. And for the birth of our two children.

Seven years ago I was alone. I was drained mentally and emotionally. I was scarred and damaged. But in the midst of it all I hadn't given up on love. I don't think I realized how much I wanted to be loved until Hanif literally picked me up and helped me get back on my feet.

His mean ass was there for me in ways no one else had ever been. He was the first person to tell me he loved me and back it up with his actions. As my lover. My provider. My protector. He always says he was single and guarded for years because he had his heart on reserve. Waiting to love me. Waiting for me to be his saving Grace. And seeing as he has flourished into this… amazing, loving, carefree man who still gives no fucks and takes no shit at times, I believe him.

Seems he needed to be loved just as much as me.

And I wouldn't trade this love and happiness in for anything in the world.

Braille and Lorenzo

Lorenzo had always been a busy body, but after spending seven years in jail… it's like… he was on a Superman power trip. With him trying to build this resort and starting a black wall street here in Memphis, I didn't think we'd be able to live the normal family life for a couple of years. But when I told him I was pregnant that changed.

It's like he realized what was most important in his life. Family. Love. Me. Our baby. Although he still wanted to do both of those things, he made Loren and I his main priority. He started spending eight hours a day throughout the week on business, and the rest of the time he devoted to us.

After my last semester in school I graduated with my Masters in Nursing, and believe it or not… I quit! Watching my body grow and change because of Loren did something to me. And when she made her arrival into this world two months ago… I don't know… I just… was on some housewife shit.

There was nothing I enjoyed more than getting up, making love to my husband, and seeing to our daughter. We had more than enough money saved up because of my saving and his investments, and more would be coming in soon because of the resort and black market. So… I too realigned my priorities and gave myself completely to my family.

I figured maybe one day when Loren was older that I would return to nursing. But now… all I wanted to do was enjoy my family. Everything else could wait. We'd waited so long to get back to us… and nothing was going to stand in the way of that.

Jessica and Vega

Only my husband would get so nervous about the birth of our baby boy Vinci that he would pass out. Not just in the house when I told him that my water broke, but during delivery. Now, his ass was laid up in a bed next to me holding Vinci because the third time he passed out, when he was asked to cut the umbilical cord, he hit the ground so hard they were afraid he had a concussion.

If I wasn't in such pain I would have been laughing at him the entire time, but at that moment, all I could think about was getting my little baby out of me while the big one damn near gave me multiple heart attacks.

The last time Vega woke up, though, it was to the sight of Vinci. The doctor and nurses helped him get in the bed next to me, and they gave him Vinci to hold – after they tested his vitals and made sure he was awake and present enough to hold him.

And as I watched him hold Vinci, I realized at that moment, that everything I'd gone through in my past made this moment. It made my character. It gave me strength. It pushed me into Vega's arms with a desire for love and normalcy.

Yes, my father was absent in my life. Yes, I had to watch my sister love and lose. Kill herself because of her love for a man. Yes, I was raped. Yes, I feared love. Yes, I feared loss. But my God... what I've gained...

What I've gained is priceless.

All because I let go and I opened up.

Vega ran his thumb over Vinci's small hand and looked over at me with a smile before standing and walking over to me. He kissed me sweetly then rested his forehead on mine.

"I love you, Jess."

"I love you too."

"Thank you for him. For us. For giving me the chance to love you."

"Thank you for wanting and choosing to. Thank you for not giving up on me."

He kissed me again as the door creaked open slowly. I broke away from him and looked at the door. I rolled my eyes and shook my head. There was no way in hell my doctor was going to let my parents, Jabari, Christina, Power, Elle, Rule, Camryn, my play sisters Alayziah and Layyah, Braille, Lorenzo, baby Loren, Grace, Hanif, Hosea and Neema, and Vega's parents stay in my room.

I don't even know how they all were able to get past the nurses' station! Probably a connect Braille had from working here in the past.

All I could do was laugh as they all huddled into the room around us. The room swelled with love and tears immediately filled my eyes.

With all of the change that occurred in my life over the years... letting go of emotional baggage, graduating college and landing my dream job as a talk show host, falling in love and marrying the man of my unknown dreams, and working towards having my own production company and network... I'd adapted a quote that I recited every morning and night after saying my prayers - Man cannot discover new oceans unless he has the courage to lose sight of the shore. For years, I let fear keep me from living. Fear of loving. Fear of losing. Fear of being rejected. Fear of being hurt.

But no more.

My heart had been broken, love was put on hold... but now it's open. Now, I'm discovering new love. New levels in life. New oceans. *Definitely* new and vast and deep oceans.

THE END

CPSIA information can be obtained
at www.ICGtesting.com
Printed in the USA
LVHW02s2340070818
586327LV00009B/322/P